RED ROOFS & OTHER STORIES

MICHIGAN MONOGRAPH SERIES IN JAPANESE STUDIES

NUMBER 79

CENTER FOR JAPANESE STUDIES
UNIVERSITY OF MICHIGAN

RED ROOFS
& OTHER STORIES

by Tanizaki Jun'ichirō

Translated by
Anthony H. Chambers
and Paul McCarthy

University of Michigan Press
ANN ARBOR

The original titles of these stories, in the order in which they appear in this collection, are: "Tomoda to Matsunaga no hanashi" (1926), "Shinwai no yo" (1919), "Majutsushi" (1917), and "Akai yane" (1925).

To the memory of the late Donald Richie, and to Burton Watson, our mutual friends and mentors.

CONTENTS

The stories in this volume—here translated into English for the first time—date from 1917 to 1926, spanning the first and second decades of Tanizaki's fifty-five-year career. After bursting onto the Tokyo literary scene in 1910 with "The Tattooer" and publishing a number of other dazzling stories and plays over the next few years, Tanizaki experienced something of a slump, roughly from 1914 to 1923. A few gems from this period stand out, nonetheless, including some brilliant stories (e.g., "Two Acolytes," 1918, and "The Thief," 1921) and Tanizaki's best play, *Okuni and Gohei* (1922). At the same time, Tanizaki strove in these years to reinvent himself, experimenting with autobiographical fiction ("Sorrows of a Heretic," 1917), "a poem in prose" ("The Magician," 1917, included here), Chinoiserie (e.g., "A Night in Qinhuai," 1919, also included here), detective fiction (e.g., "On the Road," 1920), and film scenarios composed for a Yokohama studio (e.g., *A Serpent's Lust*, 1922).

Tanizaki was thirty-eight in 1924 when he emerged from his slump with the seminal *Naomi*, his first fully successful novel. Two stories in the present volume date from the years right after *Naomi*—"Red Roofs," in 1925, and "The Strange Case of Tomoda and Matsunaga," 1926, when Tanizaki was reaching full stride in the period that culminated with such masterworks as *Some Prefer Nettles* (1928) and *A Portrait of Shunkin* (1933). *Naomi* and its successors are relatively free of the posturing that characterizes many of the works of the preceding decade, but several elemental themes persist: masochism, a fascination with women—especially "bad" ones—and exoticism.

This collection opens with "The Strange Case of Tomoda and Matsunaga," whose title and theme suggest the influence of Robert Louis Stevenson's *The Strange Case of Dr Jekyll and Mr Hyde*. The exotic Other appears in several distinct forms in Tanizaki. If that which is removed from us in time, though not in place, may be called "exotic" (a reasonable extension of the word, we think), then the stories set in premodern Japan (Edo, Sengoku, Heian) qualify as exotic (of the Japanese, nonmodern type). Tales like "Kirin" (1910) are both geographically and temporally exotic (Chinese, nonmodern). Stories and essays based on Tanizaki's travels in China (e.g., "A Night in Qinhuai") represent an exoticism that is contemporary and neither Japanese nor Western, and "The Gourmet Club" (1919), with its culinary eroticism, transfers this exotic/contemporary setting to Yokohama's Chinatown. It is perhaps only in "Tomoda and Matsunaga" that the West is used as an actual, if partial, setting, and here exotic women are on full display.

The story presents two cultural poles. The first is a quiet, soothing, traditional Japan, represented by the Yamato countryside, scenes at Buddhist temples in Nara, and evocations of the colors, sounds, smells, and tastes of everyday Japanese life—details that anticipate Tanizaki's famous essay *In Praise of Shadows* (1933), such as the fragrance of the morning miso soup, the quiet colors of bowls of rice, pickles, seaweed soup, and sea-bream sashimi arranged on a lacquered tray. The Yamato sections of the story constitute a kind of rough sketch or early study for the fuller portrait of Japanese aesthetics given some years later.

The other pole is the decadence of 1920s Paris, with its echoes in Shanghai and the Western-style brothels of Yokohama and Kobe. The very qualities that are extolled in *In Praise of Shadows* and the Yamato sections of the story are castigated in the "Western" sections of "Tomoda and Matsunaga" with only a slight shift in vocabulary. A room is seen not as suggestively shadowy but as dim and gloomy. Voices and tones are not restrained, modest, mysterious, with a slight cloudiness, but rather are reedy falsettos. Complexions that might have been praised as "not dead white, but with a slight yellowish overtone, giving a soft, sweet effect" are here seen as merely "yellow" and judged to be "very unpleasant." Every quality is passed before the evaluating mirror and finds itself reversed.

With the rejection of the "passive East" comes a devotion to an antithetical West. For Tomoda, the West is merely a place of physical, sensuous, and sensual experience. Specific references in the Western sections of the story are to food (chateaubriand), drink (champagne, sherry, cognac, absinthe, and vermouth), and women (voluptuous, available, and almost always fair skinned; the adjective *white* appears again and again). The West is a sphere of freedom, conceived not politically or intellectually but as a kind of unbounded psychophysical energy—freedom from family ties, from the restraints of custom, convention, and morality, from the tyranny of the everyday. The tango and Apache dances that Tomoda so energetically performs with the foreign women in the Yokohama brothels represent this aspect of wild abandon.

In short, the West exists here, as in much of Tanizaki's fiction, as an almost purely subjective construct, something to set over against other things—the Japanese, the traditional, or the everyday world of most of his characters (and assumed readers). It is an object of fantasy or imagination, significant not in itself but as it works upon the characters and is worked upon by them.

In fact, Tanizaki never traveled in the West, but he visited China from mid-October to early December 1918. His major stops included Tianjin, Beijing, Nanjing, Suzhou, Hangzhou, and Shanghai. As was common among Japanese travelers in China at the time, he stayed in Japanese inns, ate Japanese food, and toured with Japanese guides.

His travels inspired several stories and sketches, the most notable of which is "A Night in Qinhuai." The narrator of the story patronizes a Japanese inn in Nanjing, as Tanizaki did, but sets himself apart from other Japanese visitors by employing a Japanese-speaking Chinese guide and, as a result, is able to savor some experiences beyond the ken of most other Japanese travelers of the time. Indeed, Tanizaki did not conceal his contempt for his more ethnocentric compatriots in "An Account of Travels in Suzhou" (1919).

Much of the interest of "A Night in Qinhuai" lies in its vivid evocation of a dangerous, freewheeling Nanjing in 1918, as different from the city of today as one could imagine. A blend of the sinister, the ominous, and the erotic is characteristic of Tanizaki's work from "The Tattooer" to his late years, as in "Manganese Dioxide Dreams" (1955).

The essaylike style of "A Night in Qinhuai" has led some readers to conclude mistakenly that the work is an essay. It anticipates Tanizaki's later masterpieces in a similar style, such as "Arrowroot" (1931) and "The Reed Cutter" (1932). Tanizaki's aim in employing this narrative device, as stated in "Postscript to 'A Portrait of Shunkin'" (1934), was to "convey the greatest feeling of reality."

The style and subject matter of "The Magician" are typical of works that led some critics early in his career to pigeonhole Tanizaki, somewhat misleadingly, as a "diabolical" writer and a proponent of art for art's sake. First published with the English subtitle "A Poem in Prose," "The Magician" can be seen as an experiment in writing prose that is laden with a rich, obscure vocabulary and a superabundance of adjectives and adverbs, inspired by the style of fin-de-siècle writers in Europe. Readers who find the vocabulary of this translation recherché should rest assured that readers of the original, as well, would be likely to turn to their dictionaries more often than usual.

W. Somerset Maugham, whose work Tanizaki admired, described his novel *The Magician* (1908) in terms that the mature Tanizaki might have applied retrospectively to his own story: "The style is lush and turgid, not at all the sort of style I approve of now, but perhaps not unsuited to the subject; and there are a great many more adverbs and adjectives than I should use to-day. I fancy I must have been impressed by the écriture artiste, which the French writers of the time had not yet entirely abandoned, and unwisely sought to imitate them."[1]

A central theme in much of Tanizaki's work is stated succinctly in this passage from "The Magician": "Sages, despots, poets, and scholars alike possess hearts that are drawn to the 'mysterious.' They would probably say that they came [to see the magician] for research, for the experience, or to proselytize. Perhaps they believe so themselves. But if you ask me, in the depths of their souls lurks a nature that, in varying degrees, feels beauty as I feel it and dreams the same dreams as I do. The only difference is that, unlike me, they are unaware of the beauty and the dreams, or do not affirm them." Tanizaki's penchant, here and elsewhere, for writing about dreams and fantasies is reflected in the lover's description of the narrator as one "who prefer[s] demons and monsters to humans, who live[s] more in hallucinations than in reality."

Amorality, another common Tanizaki theme, is extolled at the end of the story, when the narrator exclaims, "[T]he agony of human conscience disappeared completely, and a joy as bright as the sun and as wide as the sea gushed forth inexhaustibly," but, characteristically, his ecstasy is interrupted by the real world, in the form of his no-nonsense "former lover," who demands, "I've come to take back my lover. . . . [R]eturn him to me immediately."

Following the Great Kantō Earthquake of 1923, Tanizaki fled west from Tokyo and lived for many years in Kyoto and the suburbs between Osaka and Kobe, where "Red Roofs" (1925) is set. The title refers to the distinctive tile roofs of Culture Homes (*bunka jūtaku*), that is, "modern" houses, which proliferated in those suburbs in the first three decades of the twentieth century. Reflecting the gradual adaptation of Western design to Japanese life, these structures, intended for the urban middle class, typically featured a Western ex-

---

1. "A Fragment of an Autobiography," in *The Magician* (London: Heinemann, 1956).

terior and a Japanese interior, often with the addition of a Western-style parlor. The protagonists of *Naomi* rent such a house, which Jōji introduces this way: "Modern and simple, it was, I suppose, what people would nowadays call a 'Culture Home' though the term was not yet in vogue then. More than half of it consisted of a steep roof covered with red slate."[2]

Tor Road, where "Red Roofs" opens, led visitors from the wharfs of Kobe uphill to the Tor Hotel and the surrounding neighborhood (Kitano-chō), where many Europeans and Americans lived. The road was lined with fashionable shops meant to appeal to Westerners and Japanese who aspired to a "Western" way of life. Suikōen (pine fragrance gardens) Culture Village, where the protagonist lives, appears to have been inspired by Kōroen (smoke-tree fragrance gardens), near Kobe.

As Chiba Shunji has pointed out, "Red Roofs" appeared right after *Naomi* "and can be seen as a depiction of the anatomy of a masochist from Naomi's point of view."[3] Readers will immediately recognize affinities between the two works and will see, as well, that "Red Roofs" anticipates *Some Prefer Nettles* and *Quicksand* (1928–1930), also set in towns between Osaka and Kobe, novels that depict the "privacy, the freedom, and the new life-styles possible in the suburbs."[4]

Among the freedoms afforded by these new suburbs was the freedom—at least in the author's imagination—to pursue unconventional sexual relationships. Like *Naomi*, "Red Roofs" deviates from conventional, early-twentieth-century Japanese conceptions of sexuality by displaying a woman's sexual desires. The conventional Japanese paradigm, which remained firmly in place well into the twentieth century, conceived of sexuality exclusively from the male point of view: males having sex with women and males having sex with males (*joshoku, nanshoku*). Mayuko's aggressive pursuit of sex-

---

2. *Naomi*, translated by Anthony H. Chambers (New York: Knopf, 1985).

3. *Jun'ichirō rabirinsu II*, "Kaisetsu," p. 287.

4. Ken K. Ito, *Visions of Desire*, p. 115.

ual gratification with Teramoto, Onchi, and other handsome young men in "Red Roofs" offers a notable break from the traditional male-centered paradigm.

"Red Roofs" is unusual among Tanizaki's works also in that it is narrated from a woman's point of view—and a sexually predatory woman at that. In a reversal of the standard formula, male characters become eroticized sex objects. Early-twentieth-century Japanese authors eroticized women's bodies as much as the censors would allow, but the erotic longing with which Teramoto's and Onchi's bodies are evoked in "Red Roofs" is a departure even from *Naomi*, none of whose men is depicted in flattering terms, and from most of Tanizaki's other work. Representations of homoerotic feelings in a middle-aged man are rare in the mainstream of early-twentieth-century Japanese literature as well, but they are present here in the portrait of Mayuko's masochistic patron, Odagiri.

References to Japan's fledgling film industry (which, like Tanizaki himself, relocated to Kyoto after the 1923 earthquake) reflect Tanizaki's experience as a screenwriter in Yokohama in 1920 and 1921. Though "Red Roofs" has apparently never been made into a film (unlike *Naomi*, which has been adapted at least four times), the strikingly visual quality of the story is probably due to the author's fascination with film.

AHC & PMcC

Names and ages are given in the Japanese style: family name precedes given name; and the calendar years in which one has lived are counted, rather than the number of full years elapsed since the day of birth.

THE STRANGE CASE OF

TOMODA AND MATSUNAGA

Translated by Paul McCarthy

PART 1

It was some five or six years ago, on August 25, 1920, to be exact, that I received a letter from a lady as yet unknown to me—"Shigeko," from the Yamato area. I am able to give the exact date because I still have that letter. Actually, a great many letters from previously unknown "literary youths and girls" come to me. If I happen to be busy, I haven't the time to read through them all and just bundle them in a corner of my study, where they sometimes lie completely forgotten. Yet in the case of Shigeko's letter, I found myself, for once, wanting to open and read it immediately. The characters on the envelope were written not in pen and ink but with a brush in an old-fashioned, elegant style. The look of the return address—"Shigeko, care of Matsunaga Gisuke of Aza XX, Yagyumura, Soekami District, Yamato"—suggested at once that this was not the letter of some ordinary literary young lady.

The letter is rather long, but it touches on the essence of this story, so I will go to the trouble of reproducing it here.

Esteemed Sir,
    At this time of great heat, I trust that you and the members of your family are nonetheless in ever-increasing good health, and offer you my felicitations. I am, as indicated below, the wife of a person named Matsunaga Gisuke,

residing in Yagyumura in Yamato. I know it is the height of rudeness for me, who has not had the honor of meeting you, suddenly to send you a letter of this kind; but since there are various deep matters connected with it, I most humbly and earnestly beg the favor of your listening to my story.

I married into the Matsunaga family in 1905 when my husband was twenty-five and I eighteen. My husband Gisuke was the eldest son and had spent several years studying in Tokyo prior to our marriage, having graduated from Waseda University.

The family had been engaged in agriculture for many generations, and even after our marriage, my husband had no particular occupation to devote himself to. We spent the first half year as a happily married couple, but after the death of his aged mother in the following winter, there was a gradual change in my husband's behavior. He began to treat me harshly and would rant about how there was no point in growing old and decrepit in such a god-forsaken, out-of-the-way place. He started to go from time to time to Kyoto and Osaka to relieve his melancholy. Then the next year, in the summer of 1906, just when I had become pregnant, my husband seemed for some reason to have come to a firm decision: He would go to the Occident for one or two years, he declared, and then he promptly set off on his overseas journey. I, of course, and all the rest of the family were greatly opposed to his plan and had done our best to dissuade him at the time, but to no avail.

No word whatsoever came to us from my husband during his travels, and for some three years I looked after our firstborn daughter, Taeko. I was extremely worried about what could have happened to him when, without advance word of any kind, he suddenly returned home in the autumn of 1909. He had never suffered from any major illnesses, but he did not have a very strong constitution; and it seemed to me that he must have done damage to his health during his stay abroad. His color was not good, and soon after his return he showed signs of extreme neurasthenia. For nearly three years, until the late spring of 1912, he stayed quietly at home, treating me with kindness and showing real affection for Taeko. His health improved little by little, and his neurasthenia as well. But then, that year—in the early summer of 1912, as I recall—without giving any reason why and without letting us know where he was going, he said he was leaving; but that we were not to worry because he would surely return after two or three years. During his absence, we were not to inquire as to his whereabouts for any reason whatsoever; and if we did inquire, we would not be able to locate him in any event. He urged me to take good care of our daughter and to handle any matters that might arise in his absence, and then he left. I felt compelled to do as he said—what else could I have done?

Once again after about three years, in the autumn of 1915, my husband returned. As before, he looked pale and ill and was suffering from extreme neurasthenia. He apologized for all the trouble he had caused me. He had become the kind of man easily given to tears, and he expressed his love for his wife and child. He was now sympathetic and compassionate and evidenced faith in the gods. In the spring of 1917, in particular, he took Taeko, then twelve years old, and me on the pilgrimage to the thirty-three sites sacred to the bodhisattva Kanzeon; and as a result, his physical health also began gradually to improve, it seemed to me.

I felt a quiet happiness at seeing my husband so settled in mind and was sure that nothing untoward would occur again; but when the summer of 1918 came, yet again he went off to who knows where, saying the same things to me as before. Counting from the autumn of 1915, close to three years had again passed. It has now been about two years, and next year it will be three, so I find myself anxiously waiting and hoping that he will return next year. Yet I have no idea where he has been or what he has been doing. Weak though our karmic connection may have been, he is my husband. For the sake of my second daughter as well, now two years old, I have tried to endure everything. My husband has never suggested that he leaves home because he has grown tired of me—it seems there are other reasons for his absences.

While he is home with us, he is loving toward me and does everything possible to make me happy. He even weeps when he leaves us, begging me to wait for him. And so I have no reason at all to resent him. I endure his absences, waiting patiently for his return for however many years. But our eldest daughter, Taeko, has been suffering from pleurisy since last winter, and her condition has recently become very serious, so that I feel the most intense anxiety from day to day. She often has a fever and keeps saying that she wants to see her father. I feel so sorry for her and am at a loss what to do. Our relatives have been trying to determine my husband's whereabouts ever since the last time he disappeared, and, suspecting that he went abroad again this time, they have been making inquiries on that score. But they have not found a trace of his whereabouts. Nor has there been word that anyone has seen someone resembling him in Tokyo, Kyoto, or Osaka. When I recall my husband's words to the effect that we would not be able to find him even if we tried, I feel a strange disquiet.

With regard to that, when my husband came home the last time, he had no luggage with him—only the clothes on his back and a small satchel he was carrying. And when, three years later, he left again on his travels, he took only that satchel with him. While he was staying in the country with us, he guarded it very carefully, forbidding anyone else to touch it. In fact, however, though I had no desire to pry into his secrets, there were so many things that I could not understand that, while knowing it to be wrong, I did, just once, take a peek into the satchel. Inside I found a man's gold ring set with an amethyst, a personal seal with the name "Tomoda," and a single postal card. In addition there were some souvenirs of his trip to the Occident: dozens of truly lubricious photographs of foreign women in various shocking poses.

That was all. The postal card was addressed to Mr. Tomoda Ginzō c/o Café Liberté, Ginza Owari-chō 3-chōme, Kyōbashi Ward, Tokyo, while the return address was your own. The postal card's message was: "Please forgive me for the night before last. What happened regarding the matter we were discussing? I await your reply," or words to that effect. It was written in pen and ink in a highly cursive style and dated May 7, 1913, I clearly recall. I know your distinguished name from often having seen it in newspapers and magazines, but I have no knowledge of a Tomoda Ginzō, or of why my husband should have in his possession the personal seal and a postal card belonging to Mr. Tomoda. Also, the ring is too large for my husband's finger, so I am sure it must belong to someone else. Thus, I am all the more doubtful and suspicious about the matter.

I must beg your pardon for writing at such tedious length about this, but the above is a general account of how things stand. Since my husband, Gisuke, had in his possession the postal card described above, I wondered if perhaps you might know him. Perhaps "Tomoda" might be an alias adopted by my husband . . . In my worried state, I have put all concern for courtesy aside and ventured to send you this letter. As I have already said, I have no intention of pressing to find out where my husband might be. Only, if you have some idea of his whereabouts, I would be very grateful if you would tell him the gist of what I have written to you and let him know that his daughter is very ill. I feel sure that you would be able to do so in a way acceptable to my husband—far more so than if I contacted him directly myself.

If you do not have any knowledge of Matsunaga Gisuke, then I would like to ask you what sort of person "Tomoda" might be and what his present address is.

I realize that it is very presumptuous of me to burden you, with whom I have no direct connection, with something like this; but in the present circumstances there is nothing I can do but rely upon your help, while begging your kind understanding.

I have taken the liberty of enclosing a photograph of my husband, taken when the three of us set out upon the pilgrimage to the thirty-three holy places some years ago. Normally he hated having his photo taken, but on this occasion he permitted it, saying it would be a souvenir for us. He was thirty-seven at the time and is by now forty.

Finally, I would like to ask you to keep the fact that I have sent you this letter a secret from other persons, though I know that this might not be possible, depending on circumstances. I wish to leave all such matters to your discretion and judgment as to what would be best. With the most earnest entreaties for your kind aid,

Respectfully,
Matsunaga Shigeko   August 23, 1920

The letter had been mailed on August 23 and arrived at my house in Tokyo's Aoyama district two days later, on the morning of the twenty-fifth. Slugabed that I am, I unfolded this long letter as I lay in bed on my pillows. It will hardly be necessary to say how surprised I was by its contents, and how strongly my curiosity was aroused. I felt as well that this "Shigeko" was a person of a high refinement rare in today's women. As I have already mentioned, the calligraphy was "soft" and elegant, and it covered the several-foot-long sheet of Japanese paper in a graceful way. She wrote that "the family has been engaged in agriculture for many generations"; but, in any case, it must have been a family of considerable distinction. And "Shigeko" herself would surely have acquired the cultural background appropriate to a lady. Otherwise she would never have been able to write so fluently of such things in the traditional epistolary style.

Such were my thoughts as I unfolded again the lengthy letter and read it two or three more times.

I held in my hand the enclosed photograph of the three persons, parents and child, and gazed intently at it. It was a card-sized, full-length photo of the three, dressed for the pilgrimage to the thirty-three holy places, with their woven reed hats in hand; the little girl was in the center. The faces were small and hard to see clearly, but Matsunaga Gisuke, Shigeko's husband, though said in the letter to be "thirty-seven at the time," looked much older in the photo— forty-two or -three. He was a thin, gangling, very sickly looking man whose protuberant cheekbones and harsh features made him ugly. His gaze was rather acute, but he didn't have the wise look of a man who had graduated from university and traveled abroad. He seemed at first glance to be no more than a very ordinary rural fellow. There was no need for me to wrack my brain for memories of him—I had no acquaintances who had a face like this. The name Matsunaga Gisuke was also unknown to me. I did, however, have contact with Tomoda Ginzō, but he in no way resembled the man in this photo. The two of them could hardly have been one and the same person.

As for Shigeko, who stood beside her husband in the photo, she may not have been a very great beauty, but she was a woman of gentle features with an air of refinement that did not betray the elegant impression I'd received from the superb calligraphy in her letter. The photo was of course the work of a rural photographer, so her image had been touched up in an old-fashioned way, making her seem lifeless and doll-like; but the oval face, with its small, tightly closed mouth, and the eyes which, though gentle, had a sparkle to them, suggested to me (was I only imagining it?) an intelligent individual. Then, too, her traditional pilgrim's dress made her personality seem even more graceful and appealing. She looked like the sort of refined and elegant woman pilgrim who might appear in some stage play. Taeko, the daughter wedged between her two parents, was cute, of course, but appeared almost completely doll-like: it was impossible to say whether she took after her father or her mother.

With the letter and photograph in front of me, I thought about what all this might mean. Frankly speaking, it was not only the fact of a totally unknown person named Matsunaga keeping a postcard from me hidden in his satchel that struck me as strange. Shigeko would have no way of knowing this, but I recognized the references to the amethyst ring and the dozens of licentious photos of Western women, as well as to the postcard. Unless I am very much mistaken, both the ring and those "licentious photos," together with the personal seal that was found in the satchel, most likely belonged to Tomoda Ginzō. Tomoda had been wearing an amethyst ring for the ten or so years I had known him, and in fact the stone in question was glittering on the middle finger of his left hand when I'd met him only two or three days before. And taking strange photos of women was one of his hobbies: he had dozens of such photos in his personal collection, which he often shared with me.

I concluded that, though he had nothing to do with me, this Matsunaga person must have some connection with Tomoda. If I asked Tomoda about him, he'd be sure to know something.

As I was thinking along these lines, it suddenly hit me that, though I'd known Tomoda for so many years, I actually had no clear idea of what kind of work he did or where he lived. When we met, it was usually by chance: I had never visited his house, nor he mine. Thus I didn't even know if he was a bachelor or married. I grant that it is very odd to have known someone for over ten years without learning more about him. Still, one has "drinking companions" with whom one drinks and amuses oneself with women while having no contact at all apart from that—it's not uncommon. And that's what Tomoda and I were—"drinking companions" who knew each other well when it came to liquor and women but never met apart from that.

For this reason, I could not recall ever having dealt with Tomoda on a matter of real seriousness, but I do think we occasionally exchanged simple postcards from time to time. The postcard that Shigeko found in her husband's satchel was addressed to "Mr. Tomoda Ginzō c/o Café Liberté, and the date was May 7, 1913—I might well have written him such a card. My reason for saying that is—and this is quite far in the past so my memories are not clear—that Tomoda and I were centering our drinking on the Café Liberté around that time. I never failed to see Tomoda there on an average of once every three days. So if I had for some reason sent him a postcard, not knowing his address, I would have sent it to the Café Liberté. As for the part about "What happened regarding the matter we were discussing? I await your reply"—I have no clear idea of what that was about, but I imagine it must have been something insalubrious, some discussion of having fun with women, or the like. At the time, Tomoda patronized a brothel where white women were available. It was called "Number 10" and was located in the Yamanote district of Yokohama. Occasionally he took me and two or three other drinking buddies there. The brothel had the look of a spacious Western residence for some nobleman or other, and Japanese clients could not easily gain access to the inner rooms reserved for pleasure. Tomoda, however, was a regular client, and his introduction gained us immediate access. For that reason, the curious bunch that gathered at the Café Liberté found Tomoda a very useful man to know. And when an interesting new girl came to Number 10, Tomoda would inform us right away: "Hey, there's a new one there now! Let's go take a look!" Probably the reference to "the matter we were discussing" in the postcard meant that I'd heard news of that kind and was planning to go off with him and needed to check if it was convenient for Tomoda. The only business we had with each other was matters of that kind, after all.

Later I was on close terms with the girls at Number 10 so I could go on my own without guidance from Tomoda. When I did go, Tomoda was almost always there. Number 10 was, as I have said, a splendid house with many rooms. There was some coming and going among the staff, but there were always seven or eight girls available. As was almost always the case with houses that featured white women, there was a dance floor and a bar downstairs and rooms for the girls on the second floor. The clients would first go to the dance floor or the bar and dance or drink with the girls. When I was amusing myself in the bar, Tomoda would sometimes suddenly come up behind me, shout a greeting, and give me a slap on the shoulder. Or, if I asked eagerly if Mr. Tomoda wasn't there that night, someone might say "He may be upstairs . . ."; and even as she spoke, down the stairs he'd thud, with his fat, potbellied physique reminiscent of a sumo wrestler's. He was tremendously popular with the girls, in part, no doubt, due to his openhanded generosity. He weighed some 170 pounds, had a truly impressive girth, and was a skillful speaker of English and French. He was, in addition, witty and charming, and his every gesture and expression showed him to be a man well acquainted with the ways of the pleasure quarters. At the time, he was the only Japanese who could outshine the European clients. The girls called him "Tom" rather than "Mr. Tomoda" and were very friendly to him.

One day, to tease him, I said, "Why, you've almost made this place your home, haven't you?"

"Well yes, I guess you could say that," replied Tomoda, raising a glass of champagne and gazing with a self-satisfied air at the girls who had gathered around him.

I said earlier that I didn't know what kind of work Tomoda did, and in that connection I recall how a strange rumor spread among our drinking companions due to Tomoda's ever-increasing patronage of Number 10. The gist of it was that, though he appeared to be a client, he was in fact the owner of the brothel—that he had secretly supplied the capital needed to start it up and was now running it. I don't know who started this rumor, but when you thought about it, it did not seem unreasonable. So far as I knew, there was nothing to prove the rumor false; on the contrary, there was ample evidence that it might be true. For example, the women in the problematic photo collection he so treasured were all either girls now at Number 10 or ones who had previously worked there. The reason he had so many photos was, according to Tomoda himself, that whenever a new girl came to the brothel he would take her to a private room and photograph her. But this kind of "naughtiness"—if indeed *naughtiness* is a strong enough word to describe his behavior—would seem impossible unless he had some special connection to the establishment, quite apart from his generosity and popularity with the girls. Perhaps showing me the photos and telling me the stories was his way of indirectly confessing that he was the owner of the brothel. He may have been revealing his secret to me at least. Come to think of it, he had said, "If you send me a postcard, it'd be better to address it in care of Number 10 rather than Café Liberté. That'd be faster." And so at some point I began to be convinced that he was indeed the operator or at least the investor behind the brothel.

We must once again take note of the fact that the postcard from me to Tomoda that Shigeko had discovered was dated May 7, 1913. So around 1913 the Café Liberté in Tokyo and Number 10 in Yokohama were Tomoda's bases of operations. But by August of 1920, when Shigeko's letter reached me, the Café Liberté and Number 10 were already long gone. So it was not that I didn't know Tomoda's whereabouts. He was already relying on two new bases: the Café Présantant in Ginza, for Tokyo, and the Number 27 in Yamanote for Yokohama. The Présantant was, like the Liberté, an ordinary café, while Number 27 was a brothel that featured white women, just as the earlier Number 10 had done. The Yamanote area of Yokohama had been literally demolished by the earthquake of 1923 without a trace; but had you gone straight past the old Gaiety Theater in the direction of Honmoku for seven or eight blocks and then turned right at a certain corner, you would have come to Number 27. The entire foreigners' residential district of Yamanote was full of dense greenery; it was quiet even in the daytime and had an exotic, Occidental air about it; and Number 27 was in the midst of an especially deserted, lonely spot. Its overgrown foliage, verging on wilderness, was unlikely to attract the attention of a passerby. It had probably been built when the port of Yokohama was first opened and had served as the residence of some important foreigner before becoming a brothel. It was similar to Number 10 in the number of rooms and their placement. The interior was brightly decorated, but the extensive facade had a neglected, faded air; and since it stood in such a lonely spot, the building looked as if it might be a haunted house. The girls there were all "new faces"; not a single one was a carryover from Number 10 days. Yet Tomoda was as regular a client there as he had been at Number 10, and it seemed to me that, as before, he had a special relationship with the place. And he had a great many photos of various kinds with the girls at the new place serving as models.

Yet one mysterious factor was how long Tomoda's Number 10 and Number 27 periods and his Café Liberté and Café Présantant periods continued and just when he made the shifts from one to the other. The relation of the periods to one another was not at all clear. My sense was that Tomoda's Café Liberté period extended from around 1913 to the present, during which time I met him frequently. When I trace my memories more carefully, however, I find an interval of two or three years—or perhaps three or four years—when for some reason we didn't meet. Number 10 went out of business around 1915 or –16, but Tomoda hadn't put in an appearance there for quite some time before that. "What's become of Tom? He never comes anymore!" I overheard the girls saying—it must have been around October of 1915. He stopped coming to the Café Liberté around that same time. Before too long the Liberté also closed its doors, and one or two years later, two or three blocks closer to Shimbashi, the Présantant opened. Then one night I ran into Tomoda by chance after his long absence: it must have been toward the end of 1918 or perhaps in the New Year of 1919. It was certainly in the winter, since a strong, cold wind was blowing fiercely. Then—ah yes, as I think back, it becomes clearer and clearer—when I reencountered him at the Présantant, I said to him, "Number 10's gone, old chap, and Yokohama is as dull as dishwater now!" Then Tomoda, smirking, replied, "You're not much of a novelist, are you? Not in the know about what's going on! There's a brand new place in Yokohama—a place just like Number 10 . . ." And he took me to Number 27 for my first visit that very night—or was it a bit later?

Now that I have written this much, the reader will surely have noticed something: it appears that Shigeko's husband Matsunaga and my friend Tomoda have a far deeper relationship with each other than I had at first thought. For according to Shigeko's letter, Matsunaga came back to his home village for the second time in the fall of 1915. *That person* remained in the countryside until the summer of 1918 and then left home once more. And it was during precisely this time—from the fall of 1915 to the summer of 1918—that I failed to see Tomoda even once. I didn't meet him for a period of around three years. When I realized this, I became intensely curious. Next I tried to remember when it was that I first got to know this fellow Tomoda: it was around 1908 or –9. I've forgotten who might have introduced us or whether we spoke to each other without an introduction under the influence of drink; but I think it was at the Café Kōnosu in what was then Koami-chō, Nihombashi. But I am not clear on when we would have shifted from the Café Kōnosu to the Café Liberté. At some point, Tomoda stopped coming to the Kōnosu, and then some years later he appeared one day in the Café Liberté, as I recall. Right now I cannot say for sure that the period when he hid himself from our little group for the first time was actually three years or so. However, if, as seems to be the case, Shigeko's husband returned home in the fall of 1909 and then left again toward the beginning of summer in 1912, the periods seem to match. Let's put it in the form of a table, for clarity's sake.

First Period—from summer 1906 to autumn 1909
Matsunaga Gisuke travels to the Occident
and Tomoda Ginzō appears in Café Kōnosu toward the end
of this period

Second Period—from autumn 1909 to spring 1912
Matsunaga Gisuke lives at home in the country
and Tomoda Ginzō conceals himself

Third Period—from summer 1912 to autumn 1915
Matsunaga Gisuke conceals himself
and Tomoda Ginzō frequents Café Liberté and
Number 10

Fourth Period—from autumn 1915 to summer 1918
Matsunaga Gisuke lives at home in the country
and Tomoda Ginzō conceals himself

Fifth Period—from summer 1918 to the present, 1920
Matsunaga Gisuke conceals himself
and Tomoda Ginzō frequents Café Présentant
and Number 27

With respect to the first and second periods in this table, my
memories regarding Tomoda Ginzō are not completely reliable;
but if we assume that the table is on the whole accurate, then from
1909 onward, for periods of approximately three years, whenever
Matsunaga Gisuke was at home in the countryside, Tomoda Ginzō's
whereabouts were unknown. And whenever Tomoda Ginzō appeared in Tokyo and Yokohama for three years, Matsunaga Gisuke's
whereabouts were unknown.

I'd been mulling over all these at first glance strange matters as
I lay burrowed deep in the bedclothes. I was in effect forced to mull
them over. I devised the table you see above in my head as I lay there

and pondered it. I also read Shigeko's letter over and over several more times. By now it would occur to anyone that the man who calls himself Tomoda Ginzō and the man who calls himself Matsunaga Gisuke are probably one and the same person. I drew the photo of the family in pilgrim's garb to my pillowside once more and examined it carefully. Shigeko herself had written doubtfully, "Perhaps 'Tomoda' might be an alias adopted by my husband." But the sense I got from the old-fashioned, partially retouched photograph as I looked at it now suggested not only that Matsunaga Gisuke did not resemble Tomoda Ginzō but even that the difference between the two was extreme. There was no resemblance whatsoever, whether in face or physique.

One cannot deny that there is often a difference between a photograph of something and the thing itself. And when the subject is dressed in pilgrim's garb, the whole character of the person may well look different. Yet even allowing for that, as fat a man as Tomoda could hardly look so thin in his photo. Tomoda was obese to an almost pathological degree. Matsunaga in this photograph was a thin, scrawny-looking fellow. Tomoda had a round face with cheeks so plump they seemed about to burst. Matsunaga had hollow, sunken cheeks and a sharp triangular face. They were at two opposite poles: the one was cheerful and animated looking, the other dark and gloomy. Now it sometimes happens that a man grows fat and then thin, but from the time I first met him at Kōnosu, Tomoda had always looked the same. And Matsunaga must have been thin all along, as in this photograph, for Shigeko had written that her husband "had never suffered from any major illnesses, but he did not have a very strong constitution" and that "the ring is too large for my husband's finger so I am sure it must belong to someone else." Shigeko had further written that "our relatives have been trying to determine my husband's whereabouts ever since the last time he disappeared, and, suspecting that he went abroad again this time, they have been making inquiries on that score. But they have not found a trace of his whereabouts. Nor has there been word that anyone has seen someone resembling him in Tokyo, Kyoto, or Osaka." Tomoda, on the other hand, constantly frequented the Ginza area while the Café Liberté was still in business and more recently comes all the time to the Présantant—in fact, I met him there only a couple of evenings ago. If Tomoda were the same person as Matsunaga, how could it go undiscovered? Matsunaga told his wife that she would not be able to find him even if she tried, and would he be likely to be so bold as that?

And yet, as I idly thought the matter over, tucked in among my quilts, I could find no good solution. The only thing to do was to confront Tomoda directly. I had quite a bit of business to see to that day but managed to finish it by the evening, and so I set out for the Café Présantant in Ginza to find Tomoda. If by any chance he was not there, I was sure I'd find him at Number 27 in Yokohama. Judging from past experience, finding him in such a place would be a very easy thing to do.

PART 2

The Présentant was a little out of the ordinary for a café, being small and chic. The only item on the menu was beefsteak, but that was done in the true English style, grilled over charcoal briquettes—most unusual for Tokyo. The wine was of excellent quality, not at all like the plonk served in most cafés. Naturally a café like that depended not on occasional customers but on gourmets who were "regulars."

It was a gathering place for the pleasure-loving rich, but on hot summer evenings there were many customers seeking coolness as well as refreshment. That night in particular the small café was crowded and lively. From eight until nine I waited for Tomoda to appear, eating beefsteak and drinking three glasses of French vermouth.

He didn't come, though, and the faces at the nearby tables were unknown to me.

I decided to wait until ten and, after draining the last glass of vermouth, ordered a glass of Amontillado. Anyone who has read Poe's "The Cask of Amontillado" will recognize the name, but I doubt if there are many Japanese who know what kind of wine Amontillado is. To tell the truth, I myself came to know the unforgettable flavor of this wine only recently, and it was Tomoda who introduced me to it.

"Try a glass of this, won't you? It's real Amontillado!" He told one of the waiters at the café to bring a bottle of a type I'd never seen before, from among the many that were lined up on the bar shelves.

"Have you ever had a drink of this?"

"Well, I've heard of it, but I've certainly never had any. What is this 'Amontillado' anyway?"

"It's a specialty of Spain—a true sherry. Just look at the color! Ordinary sherries are darker, while this is very clear."

As he spoke, he pointed at the almost transparent amber-colored liquid that filled the glass before me to the brim.

"This is the color of real sherry. The kind you usually drink is an English imitation, with sugar added for sweetness. This isn't a fake like that. Its sweetness comes from pure grapes, with nothing added."

"It's wonderful! I've never tasted such delicious sherry!" I cried, gazing, enchanted, at the color of this wine. The taste was of an ineffably light sweetness with a faintly bitter tinge, and the rich bouquet was redolent of a southern land.

"It's strange that a wine like this would be found in this place. Can you find it everywhere?"

"Don't be silly! It's my discovery. There were two dozen bottles in the K. Company's warehouse in Yokohama, so I let this place have one dozen, and kept the other for myself." Tomoda glowed with satisfaction.

So as I tasted the sherry that night, my doubts about Tomoda grew stronger and stronger. Precisely because we were so close, I'd never given a thought to it before, but there was really no one who seemed as open as Tomoda and yet was, in fact, so full of ambiguities. What was his past like? What kind of life had he been leading? How old was he? What university had he graduated from? If asked about these specifics, I would have had no way to reply. When Tomoda was asked such questions, he always gave unclear answers, evasive ones that could be taken to mean either yes or no. He was good at English and French, knew a lot about Western manners and customs, and was a connoisseur of Western food and drink, and so I assumed that he had been to the West, but I had never had clear confirmation of that from Tomoda himself. He sometimes spoke of having had good times in Shanghai, but he never mentioned Paris or London.

"Where did you get such good training in English and French?" I'd ask, and his casual reply would be on the order of "I didn't really get trained. I just picked the languages up in the course of buying different foreign women." "So you must have spent quite a bit of time in Europe, then," I would press him. "You don't have to go to Europe to buy foreign women, you know! If you want to see Paris, you can find it in Yokohama, or Kobe, or Shanghai!" He'd shrug off my questions with a laugh.

"All right," I said to myself, "I'm going to grab hold of Tomoda and find out for sure this time! I'll wait till ten, and if he hasn't come by then I'll go on to Yokohama." Having made up my mind, I ordered a second glass of Amontillado.

"Are you by yourself tonight? You must feel lonely," said a waiter who had been working at this café for a long time. He took a glass filled with that amber liquid from his silver tray and placed it before me.

"Yeah, no luck at all tonight for me. But this place is doing very well, isn't it?"

"Well, it's summertime and we get all sorts of customers. It makes things difficult for us, actually."

"I don't know a soul here. I've been waiting around, hoping Mr. Tomoda would come."

"Really? Could he have gone to Number 27 again tonight?" The waiter smirked and cast a glance at the clock hanging above the bar area. "It's still only 9:30—a little early for him to come trooping in here."

"I wonder if he's coming at all . . . If he doesn't, I'm planning to launch a counteroffensive in Yokohama."

"What's with Number 27 anyway? Are there some cuties there lately?"

"That's what I plan to ask Tomoda. Tokyo's so boring lately."

"Well, why don't you wait a bit longer? He hasn't been by for two nights now, so he might very well come tonight."

Just as the waiter was saying this, I yelled "Here he is!" He was wearing a linen suit and an English trilby in the Tuscan style—he was in white from head to foot. Only his face was a shiny red as befitted a drinker. Having suddenly entered through the café's front door, Tomoda's bulky frame was moving toward me.

"Hey!" Seeing me, Tomoda raised his right hand and snapped his thumb and index finger together, the way Westerners often do. He pushed his way through the crowd and plumped himself down on the chair opposite me, the white shirt over his potbelly billowing out as he did so.

"Welcome, welcome! Your arrival has been eagerly awaited, Mr. Tomoda," said the waiter.

"Really? By whom?"

"Well, not eagerly awaiting, exactly, but I've been awfully bored here all by myself."

I thought the waiter had said something he shouldn't have, so I tried to counter it with this casual remark. But even as I spoke, my eyes went to the back of Tomoda's left hand resting on the table. Tonight, again, the amethyst ring was gleaming there on his plump ring finger.

"Waiter! A gin and bitters."

"That's unusual for you," I remarked, since Tomoda hardly ever drank gin or whiskey. He only drank extremely fine claret, cognac, Rhine wine, sherry, or champagne. That was his rule—he disliked English and American liquors: "Cocktails? That's not a proper drink! A real drink should have a single, pure taste, and not be a mix of things. Americans don't know what a drink should taste like!" That was his pet theory.

"No, I don't really like gin and bitters all that much, but it's the best thing when you're feeling hot. Drink it, and you feel refreshed—the perspiration disappears."

"You don't say? Maybe I'll have one too, then."

"And it mustn't be dry gin. You've got to have Old Tom, and slip a little bitters in."

He took out his handkerchief and wiped away the sweat, globules of which were trickling down his face, as so often happens with fat people. The stiff shirt collar that he always wore was starting to wilt from the moisture.

"My God, it's hot! It's unbearable . . . Yokohama's better than this, at least."

"Oh, and what about Number 27? Anything new there?"

"You bet there is. There's a girl who came five or six days ago from Shanghai—a real looker."

" Russian, I'll bet."

"No, actually she's Portuguese, I think."

"If she's Portuguese, she must look pretty much like a Japanese."

"Listen to you—Mister Discriminating! Her eyes and hair are black, like a Japanese, but the general effect is completely Western. These Portuguese women have faces like the greatest Japanese beauties, but their bodies are well formed in the Western way. That's the general picture."

"Well, I wonder about that. You tend to exaggerate, you know."

Tomoda *did* always inflate whatever he was talking about. "There's a real stunner there," he'd say, and off you'd go, only to find she didn't amount to much.

"None of your nonsense! This one's the real thing—nothing like her up to now."

"The only way I'll know is if I get to see the goods."

"So maybe I should show you the goods . . ."

"You mean go to Yokohama right now?"

Tomoda didn't answer, but giving a cautious look around, he put his hand into the breast pocket of his jacket.

"I've got a photo right here."

"I'm surprised you've already photographed her."

"I was quick—got it as soon as she arrived. Here, take a look." He took a photo from its envelope and showed it to me, shielding it in his palm.

"Just look at this body, eh?"

"Hmm. She's still really young."

"She says she's eighteen, but I'd guess twenty. So what about it? Do you like her?"

"Yeah, of course I do—a lot! She's worth going to take a gander at."

Tomoda's chair rocked a little with his loud laughter at this remark.

"Well, lookee lookee! I thought that'd be your reaction," and he laughed again.

"As a matter of fact, Tomoda, I've got a photo I want to show you, too."

I took advantage of his laughter to stick the knife in. I put my hand into my breast pocket, just as he had.

"Yeah? And what might that be?"

"It's this!" I pulled out the photo of the Matsunaga family and slapped it down on the table.

"Why, what is this? It looks like a pilgrimage or something . . ." he managed to say, but the expression on Tomoda's face the instant he saw the photo is something I'll never forget. Forced to look at the photo, even without picking it up to get a closer view, the look on his face changed, as if every hair on his body was standing on end. His bleary, drunken eyes opened wide and had an intense, strange glitter in them, as if he were holding in some violent emotion, some inexpressible terror or pain. Dumbfounded at the look in his eyes, I fell silent. After a while I heard a "clink" and found that Tomoda had suddenly grabbed his glass and gulped down the remaining gin.

"So why are you showing me this photograph?" he finally said, but his words betrayed a rage that he could not conceal no matter how he might try.

"Don't you recognize the man in the photo?"

"No, never seen him before!"

"You have no recollection of him at all?"

"None at all."

I seemed to have gotten off to a bad start and made him angry. I decided to shift the battle lines and started to reason with him quietly and gently.

"If you don't know this man, then things are even stranger than I thought. The man in the photograph is one Matsunaga Gisuke, from Yagyumura in Yamato."

"Uh-huh. And what's so strange about that?"

"He's been missing for the last two or three years."

"Well, are you a friend of his or something?" He spoke in a biting way.

"No, I'm not a friend of his, but there's a reason I think you should know him . . ."

I felt I had to tell Tomoda briefly about the letter, even though Shigeko had asked me not to reveal this to others, if at all possible. It occurred to me to invite him for a stroll outside so we could talk; but the restaurant was noisy that night, and an electric fan was whirring away right next to our table, so there was no danger that the other customers would overhear what we might say. I took advantage of the situation and decided to pursue the subject quietly, in a well-lighted place where I could observe how the expression on his face might change.

As my tone of voice grew calmer and gentler, Tomoda little by little recovered his composure. But then, in the middle of my story, he abruptly summoned the waiter and had him bring some absinthe to the table. Grunting, he brought the liqueur to his lips again and again. It was as unusual for him to drink absinthe as to drink gin bitters, both being very strong types of liquor. It was clear to me that he was trying to pile greater, more violent drunkenness on his already drunken state. As I proceeded with my story, his "uh-huh" responses grew more enthusiastic, and his eyes began to gleam with curiosity.

When he had heard me out, he thumped the table, exclaiming

with his usual heartiness, "Now I call that interesting! Why, it's a regular detective story!"

"What do you mean, 'a regular detective story'? So you do recognize the fellow?"

"No, I don't know the man himself, but I do recall the things you say he had in his bag. They're mine, for sure—the seal, the ring, the photos."

"You don't say? But then, why is this fellow in possession of them?"

"My bag was stolen from me."

"Really? Is that so? Stolen, you say?"

"Yes, let's see . . . when would it have been? If that postcard was in the bag, it must have been . . . Yes, it was stolen when I was staying at the XXX Hotel in Hakone.

"The bag itself could be mine, in fact."

"Shigeko wrote in her letter that it was a small handbag sort of thing."

"That's right. It was just an ordinary, everyday sort of boxy satchel. I don't recall whether the postcard from you was in the satchel or not, but I had the photographs and the seal and the ring in it for sure. And there were two or three hundred yen as well, but it was all taken."

"Did they catch the thief?"

"No, they didn't. I didn't want to make it public, so I never reported the theft to the police. It wasn't much money, after all, and it would have been awkward for me if those photographs ever came to light."

"Then what about that ring you have on now?"

"I had it made after the theft, to look just like the old one." He paused, thought a moment, and added, "It's odd, actually, to have one's ring stolen; but I have this strong dislike of thunder, and when I hear it, I take off anything metallic I have on me—a ring, a watch, whatever. Anyway, I ran into a terrible thunderstorm in Hakone that evening, so I took my ring off and put it in the satchel. I forgot all about it, went to bed, and found my satchel had been stolen while I slept."

"So this Matsunaga fellow might be a thief? The letter from Shigeko was very well written, and Matsunaga would seem to be a man of quite good family."

"But don't you think it's odd for someone to leave home every few years? Those photographs might appeal to people of certain tastes, and someone might well want that postcard, too, if he were an admirer of your fiction. So the stolen items might have passed through several hands until they came to Matsunaga. But still, the business about the seal and the ring is very strange."

"Perhaps he used up all the money he stole and, fearing that the other items would be traceable, put them away for safekeeping."

"That's it! That must be what happened."

"But in that case, isn't it odd that he would keep the postcard from me? He would have burnt it or ripped it into little pieces."

"I know why: the thief was a fan of yours!" he said, roaring with laughter.

"What an awful conclusion to reach!"

"I suppose even a thief might read your novels if he were a man of some education." Another hearty laugh.

"Well, that really does put me in a fix. How should I reply to Shigeko then? I'd feel awfully bad for her, calling her husband a thief. And who knows how much resentment that would provoke? I'll have to watch what I say."

"Why not just tell her you don't know anything about the matter? I have no regrets about the stolen items at this point."

"But I have to say something about you, after all!"

"Why so?"

"Shigeko wrote, 'If you do not have any knowledge of Matsunaga Gisuke, then I would like to ask you what sort of person "Tomoda" might be, and what his present address is . . .'"

"Never! I want absolutely nothing to do with this whole business!" Tomoda suddenly shouted, and once again he grew terribly pale.

"But given the existence of that postcard, how can I say that I don't even know anyone named Tomoda Ginzō?"

"All right, then tell her that you do know Tomoda Ginzō and asked him about the matter, but he said he has nothing whatsoever to do with any Matsunaga Gisuke.

"As for the contents of that satchel, the postcard might have been his, but he has no knowledge of any of the other things. Tomoda Ginzō has never lost his personal seal.

"He therefore finds it very strange indeed that this Matsunaga Gisuke person should be in possession of such a postcard and seal. Tell her that!"

"Oh, but I have to give her a more detailed explanation than that or she'll never accept the situation. It's troublesome for you, I know, but Shigeko thinks that you yourself are Matsunaga and Tomoda is just an alias."

"D-d-don't be ridiculous! Just compare that photograph with me, here before you."

I gave a hearty laugh, so he wouldn't think I had any ulterior motive, and then went on: "I know that, of course; but Shigeko doesn't know you, so no wonder she has her doubts."

"Well, show me the photograph again so I can see how he looks." Tomoda picked up the photograph, and as he did so, I saw a strange terror in his eyes—not as obvious as before but clearly showing that he was fearful of something.

"Hmm . . . This is Matsunaga, eh? . . . He's a lot older than I am."

"Apparently it was taken when he was thirty-seven, but he'd be forty now."

"Then I'm four years younger than he is. I'm thirty-six this year." It was the first time he'd ever clearly revealed anything about himself.

"Really? You're thirty-six?"

"That's right. Thirty-six—born in the year of the cock, 1885. Why? Don't I look thirty-six?"

"Your face looks that young, but your hair is getting pretty thin."

"That's because I drink! People who drink tend to have problems here," he replied, pinching the top of his head. "They lose their hair early. I'm worried that I might be getting bald myself. I'm quite pessimistic about it."

"Well, your hair may be thinning, but you certainly do look four or five years younger than this fellow—that I guarantee you."

"It's not just our ages. We're not alike in any way!"

"You're not, I know. And that's what makes things so difficult."

"What do you mean by that?"

"Well, if there were any evidence that you and this man are the same person, then things would make sense; but that's not the case, so I don't know what to do."

I answered, and laughed again. In truth, though, it was no laughing matter, since the more I looked at the Matsunaga in the photograph and at the Tomoda who stood before me the more obvious the differences between them became, unfortunately.

"Look, let's handle it this way," said Tomoda, leaning over the table. "We've got to convince her that this man and I are entirely separate individuals who bear no resemblance to one another. So let's send her some recent photographs of me. Then she should have no complaints."

"Yes, that might be the simplest way."

"I'll send you some photos by post the first thing tomorrow—two or three that show me as I am. Then you send them on to her and tell her that this is Tomoda Ginzō, one look at them should clear up her doubts, and so you think there's no need to inform her of Tomoda's address or personal situation. That should take care of matters."

I had no choice but to fall in with this plausible suggestion of Tomoda's. We continued our conversation over many more drinks; but he still seemed uneasy somehow, casting occasional furtive glances at the figures of the Matsunaga family in the photograph, which lay on the table. And I let the photo sit there for a very long time, intentionally.

"How about coming to Yokohama with me now?" It was nearly eleven o'clock when he got up from the table with these words.

"I don't know . . . I've been rather busy lately."

"Oh, come along with me. I'll show you the Portuguese girl."

"I want to see her, of course, but let's make it another time. Oh, and you won't forget to send me those photos, will you?"

"Of course. I'll send them on for sure, so don't go and write that woman something you shouldn't."

We left the Présentant and walked together along the Ginza toward Shibaguchi. Both of us fell oddly silent as we left the restaurant. Tomoda seemed to be lost in thoughts of his own. And I, in mine . . . I had had too much to drink that evening and was more drunk than usual. My drunkenness made me mull over our earlier conversation with an almost obsessive persistence. This man "Tomoda" now walking beside me, who was he, in reality? His account of the stolen satchel provided a sort of explanation, but why had that look of terror come into his eyes when he was shown the photo of Matsunaga? Why had he been so eager to get drunk, or to appear drunk? And why didn't he want his identity or address made known, even though he knew his identity was being placed in doubt? The more I thought about these matters, the deeper grew the cloud of puzzling questions enveloping Tomoda. He had said earlier that Matsunaga's self-concealment every few years was suspicious, but if that was "suspicious," so was Tomoda himself. I had said jokingly, "If there was any evidence that you and this man are the same person, then things would make sense"; but in fact I was far from joking. Even if the two were not the same person, they must at least be maintaining some sort of secret contact. Hadn't Tomoda gotten to know this Matsunaga fellow on one of his trips to Europe? And might they not since then have been meeting in Tokyo every few years to engage jointly in some wicked activity, sticking as close to each other as a shadow does to a body?

"Goodbye, then," Tomoda said as we came to the Shibaguchi tram stop, with an odd brusqueness in his manner. He turned into a side street and disappeared in the direction of Shimbashi Station.

Despite what he'd said, would Tomoda really send on the photographs? Wasn't that promise just another trick of his? I had my doubts, but indeed the photos did arrive in the afternoon of the day after next. "As promised, I am sending these clear photographs of myself," he wrote in the accompanying note. "I had thought to send ordinary recent photos but couldn't find any I liked, so I had these three specially taken to serve as evidence of my appearance. One of them shows my entire person, one the upper half of my body, and one is an enlargement of my face alone. I think these should suffice, so please send all three on to that woman and touch as little as possible on anything else. I don't want her to know my address, in particular." And later in the same note he made a point of saying, "I don't like to have my address and status known to just anybody. All the more so in this case, since there is nothing to gain and perhaps something to lose by informing this woman of them. There is no need whatsoever to do so."

The three photos that he'd sent me, having been taken especially for that purpose, were faithful to his actual appearance. No better identity photographs could be imagined: general appearance, character, body type, shapes of the face and cranium, and other, more detailed features were all clear. I did notice one thing, however: whether in the full body or the upper-half-body photos, the ring did not appear, despite the fact that his hands were showing. Clearly, he had removed it to have these photos taken. "You mustn't write anything about the ring," he had said; and now he had taken great care that it would not appear in these photos, which may have been newly taken precisely for that reason.

I immediately placed these "proofs of identity" into an envelope and sent them off to Shigeko, along with my reply. My letter, however, was not written in the way Tomoda had demanded. The reason was that I had more sympathy for Shigeko than for Tomoda in the matter. Then, too, I myself had strong doubts about Tomoda's story, and I could not suppress them and tell lies to Shigeko, no matter what problems my honesty might cause me later. So I wrote her an even longer letter than the one she had sent me, recording everything I knew about this strange person, Tomoda, for her reference. I included a chronology divided into five parts to illustrate the way in which every third or fourth year brought a change in the whereabouts of both Tomoda and Matsunaga. I also reported my conversation with Tomoda at Présentant on the evening of the twenty-fifth. I gave her all this detailed information as a matter of course, and added, "I wonder what your own impressions are, looking at the enclosed photographs? And whether the photos bear any resemblance to your husband? Please do not hesitate to let me know if I can be of any help to you in your quest to resolve these and any other doubts you may have. That would enable me to pursue the inquiry further at this end. I would like to be of as much help to you as my feeble powers permit."

Four or five days later I received a letter from Shigeko expressing warm gratitude for my goodwill. To my amazement, however, she also wrote, even after having inspected the photographs, "On the basis of what you have said, I think that 'Tomoda' must be an alias being used by my husband, Matsunaga Gisuke." This letter was written in the same classical epistolary style as the first one, but I will give only the gist of it here: "In the photographs you kindly sent me, Mr. Tomoda looks unquestionably like a different person than my husband. And yet, though it may be a delusion on my part, I can't rid myself of the thought that there is something about the eyes in that round face that reminds me of my husband. He has always been thin, and so, if Mr. Tomoda has been stout all along, then there would seem to be no basis for doubt, and I myself cannot solve the riddle.

Still, I feel somehow that he might just be the same person—if my husband were four or five years younger, and if he were stouter than he has been, that might be the kind of face he would have . . . I wonder how tall Mr. Tomoda is? My husband is five foot six inches tall. And if you know where he was born, what his profession is, whether he has a wife and children, his true age, whether the story of the theft of his satchel is true or false, I would be grateful for that information. It is truly presumptuous of me to ask for your help this way, but I find myself needing to take advantage of your kind offer. My daughter's illness has gotten worse, and she keeps saying she wants to see her father. I would like you somehow to convey this news to Mr. Tomoda, if at all possible."

Having read this, I sat dazed for a time. Was it all Shigeko's delusion? Or had Tomoda managed skillfully to disguise himself so thoroughly? Would such a thing even be possible? I had run up against still greater doubts.

PART 3

My first meeting with Tomoda after receiving Shigeko's second let-ter was at the beginning of September—the first or second of the month, I believe. This time the place was not Café Présantant but Number 27 in Yokohama.

I was fairly sure I would encounter Tomoda if I went there that evening, and that was my main reason for going; but I made a show of "just having come for a bit of fun." As usual, I got a taxi from Sakuragi-chō, went from Yamashita-chō past the French consulate and up Yato Hill, arriving in front of that house in the depths of a dark, unfrequented side street around nine in the evening.

I pressed the tip of my walking stick against the call button high on the outside wall and heard a faint ring from within, from a room a little distant from the tightly closed door. The house was extremely quiet, and the ring of the distant bell sounded uncanny, as if one had tossed a stone into an empty valley—or rather, perhaps, like the work of some ghost living in a deserted house.

A Filipino houseboy came, drew back a heavy iron bolt, and opened the door by barely an inch. Peering through the darkness, he stared at the visitor standing beneath the weak light above the door.

"Good evening. It's me . . ."

"Oh, yes sir, good evening."

The houseboy normally used English, but he often tried out his clumsy Japanese on me. Realizing it was me, he opened the door just enough for me to slip through.

"You not come for long while, sir."

"Yeah, it was so damn hot . . . But I hear you've got a new girl here now. I've come to take a look at her."

"Yes, she here. One you not know here now."

"Good-looking, is she?"

"Yes, she looking very good. You like her for sure, sir." In the darkness, the Filipino's teeth flashed a smile white as the linen jacket he was wearing.

"There's another guest here now, isn't there?"

Hot though it was, the venetian blinds were down, but from between two slats in the dance hall window, a single shaft of light emerged.

"Who is it? Mr. Tom?"

"Yes. Mr. Tom only."

"Really? On his own, eh? Well, I suppose I can go in then."

"Excellent!" I thought to myself. Moving from the entranceway into the corridor, I knocked on the door of the dance hall, immediately to the left.

"Ah, you're here!" When I entered the room, Tomoda/"Tom" was sitting on a divan next to the piano, wearing a sailor's jacket, and with Catherine, in a blazing crimson crepe-de-chine dress, perched on his knee. To tell the truth, though, it was only later that I realized the dress was "a blazing crimson": at first, it looked darkish in color. The reason was that the lights in this room were designed to shift from red to white to blue; and, at the time I entered, the room was filled with a reddish light. To my eyes, used to the darkness outside, this strange soft light was very pleasant. For reasons of my own, however, no sooner had I entered the room than I turned the switch from "red" to "white."

"Oh my! Why are you making it so bright in here?" cried Catherine, shrieking with laughter—perhaps she was drunk. She was a petite, shapely woman, English, and the youngest and most popular of the girls there. In front of her stood Rosa, wearing a dress of blue georgette. Then there was another girl, dressed in light orange organdy, sitting at the piano, whom I'd never seen before. She must be the Portuguese who'd only just come to the place, I thought. Her face was not as pretty as Catherine's, but her shoulders were extraordinarily beautiful.

"Oh, let it be," laughed Tomoda. "Leave it nice and bright! There's something he especially wants to see tonight." He looked from my face to the Portuguese girl's.

"You're embarrassing me!" I laughed in my turn, speaking in Japanese. "This is the one in the photo from the other day?"

"Yeah, this is her. I'll introduce you . . ." Then, shifting into English, "Ehh, this is a Japanese gentleman, the famous novelist F. K. And this is the Portuguese beauty Edna, recently arrived from Shanghai."

"Ah so? You are novelist?" Edna stood up and came toward us.

"That's right. He's a famous Japanese novelist. Why don't you have him write about you in a novel?"

"Where in Shanghai were you?" I asked.

"I was in the French Concession."

"So you worked in one of the cafés in that area?"

"Oh, no, I wasn't working in a place like that! I was a nice girl while I was in Shanghai."

"And did you turn into a naughty girl after coming to Japan?"

"Hey, how about offering her some champagne now that you're getting to know each other?" This was from Rosa, a woman well into middle age, unpleasantly oily looking and with arms as thick as my legs. She spoke fluent French and German but was, unless my judgment is much mistaken, almost certainly a Russian Jewess. She had very few customers and was always hanging around the dance area, skillfully cadging drinks.

"Good evening!" Another girl could be heard descending the staircase, and soon Flora appeared, all in white.

"Why, Flora, you're here too!"

"Yes, it was boring down here so I went upstairs for a while . . . Bring another champagne glass for me, garçon! Maria's been taken to the Fujiya Hotel in Hakone by an American gentleman."

"And what about Emmy?"

"Emmy's gone off somewhere cooler as well. There's just the four of us left here!"

"Why, Mr. K., you sound like a policeman conducting an investigation!" Catherine was swinging her legs like some spoiled child as she lifted a champagne glass in one hand.

"Well, sure. There's not much difference between a novelist and a cop," Tomoda put in.

"Why do you say that?"

"Because it's true. They both love to find out all about other people." Was he being sarcastic at my expense? At any rate, he threw himself back in his chair with a loud laugh.

"Now that's not true, but the place seems awfully dead tonight. Are you the only customer?"

"Yup, just me. Summer's not a good time for a business like this."

"Yet you come every night, don't you?"

"I'd rather have fun with these girls than go off to some resort to escape the heat.

"There're no other customers, so the place is all mine every night. I take advantage of the summer slump to get just as drunk and wild as I like!"

"Say, Tom, we're out of champagne! Won't you get us some more?" Rosa was once again urging drinks on us.

"All right! And let's have music—play something for us!"

No sooner had Tomoda shouted this than he rose from his seat and lifted Catherine up into the air with both hands. She kept her grasp on the champagne glass, raising the hand that held it high. Tomoda traced a circle, walking on his heels, and started to make the scarlet-garbed Catherine, champagne and all, turn like a waterwheel.

"Oh, oh, Tom, let me have my drink in peace, will you!" screamed Catherine in a sharp, shrill voice no Japanese could hope to imitate.

"Why don't you try tangoing with Catherine, Tom?" It was Flora who spoke as she turned to the piano and started to play a tango.

"A tango? Why not? Hey, K., have you ever seen me tango?"

"I don't know anything about the tango . . ."

"Well, then, take a good look—this is how it's done."

The woman's body, which had been floating in air, was swept down to the ground with one slow, expansive gesture; but as soon as she touched the floor, Catherine sprang to her feet, grasped Tomoda's hand, and began to tango. I had in fact seen Tomoda dance any number of times and knew that he was a skillful dancer, but this was the first time I had seen him tango. In fact, apart from motion pictures, I had never seen the tango performed, even by Westerners. So I was amazed to see a Japanese—albeit one like Tomoda—able to dance it so well.

The man placed his hand on the woman's slim back and tightly embraced her. Then, taking her right hand in his left, he extended their two arms, pressed tightly together as if they were one, and walked forward with hips swaying. Now moving slowly, now quickly, sometimes changing suddenly to a wild, violent sort of dance—through it all, the woman's body was pressed tightly against the man's, never moving away from it. When the man took a step, the woman's leg overlaid his leg's shadow. When the man turned his body in a certain direction, the woman turned as well, her body coiled around his. The two of them seemed like a well-sewn robe: if the man was the white outer side, the woman was the scarlet lining. It looked as if Tomoda was used to dancing like this all the time, with Catherine as his constant partner. Fat though he was, when it came to dancing, Tomoda was light on his feet; and Catherine, drawn along by him, breathing in concert with him, seemed hardly to touch the ground. She appeared to have forgotten even that she was dancing, as she whirled about in a state that excluded all thought and feeling, leaning against her partner's chest as if intoxicated. The dance became more and more passionate, more and more fierce, as the couple moved away from each other to left and right and then came together again, moved away and came together. After the man pressed the woman down sideways and then, embracing her, drew her up, he touched her with the end of one finger, as if he were landing a huge fish. Then the woman would twirl about some five or six times and once again allow her whole body to sag, facing up. Her short chestnut-colored hair had a sheen that shimmered in the light, and her face suddenly flushed red, perhaps from the champagne.

Tomoda danced one dance after another, and between the dances he gulped down drink after drink of all types. Clearly he was becoming drunk, and this extreme, strangely hurried sort of drunkenness was just the same as when I had met him at Présantant.

"God, I'm tired," he cried, giving a great sigh as he threw himself heavily onto a chair. No sooner was he seated than he pulled Flora onto his lap and embraced her.

"What's that you're drinking, Tom?"

"Benedictine . . ."

"Let me have a glass!" Flora gazed up at him with her mouth slightly open and then transferred the cigarette she held between her lips to Tomoda's, the wrong way round.

"Tchu—this's awfully strong tobacco!"

"If it's too strong, don't smoke it—I will!"

"No, give it to me. Pretty please!"

Tomoda shook his head from side to side as he said this in a spoiled-child's sort of voice; then he turned to look at me with eyes bleary from drink.

"So, what do you think of my tango, Mr. K.?"

"It's really something."

"I don't know what you mean by that. You have to tell me if I'm good or not."

"You're good—I'm impressed!"

"Great! If you're impressed then have a drink."

"Oh no, I've already had too much to drink."

"Too much already?" Tomoda gave a loud and foolish laugh.

"But where did you learn the tango, anyway?"

"Well, I worked very hard to learn it, let me tell you. I didn't take lessons or anything—it's the result of all my misspent nights in cafés and cabarets!"

"When was that?"

"A long time ago."

"While you were in Europe?"

"Don't talk such nonsense. I hate to admit it, but I've never been to Europe."

"But it couldn't have been in Japan—did you learn the tango in Shanghai, say?"

"Hey, hey—don't turn policeman on me now!" Again a loud, long laugh.

I had been wanting to raise the matter of Shigeko and Yagyumura with Tomoda if I had the chance; but, while acting dead drunk, he managed never to give me an opening. Rosa was sitting right next to him, while Catherine stood behind his chair and, stretching one arm down, was holding hands with Flora. With the three women entwined there, Tomoda looked as if he were buried in bouquets of flowers and amused himself by passing his glass of liqueur first to one, then to another. Yet he never let his guard down: the evidence was that whenever I was on the point of saying something, he would stand up and say, "Come, Flora—Let's do an apache dance!" Opening his arms wide, he would begin unsteadily to dance.

I must stop here to explain about Tomoda's strange way of amusing himself: it was not only that night—he was in the habit of taking liberties of this sort whenever he came to Number 27. Part of the reason was that the women played up to him and let him do whatever he wished; but it was also the case that he himself enjoyed having a noisy old time of it with a number of companions when he drank—he liked to amuse himself in a lively, showy way. It didn't have to be any one girl in particular. He came to Number 27 to kill time, not primarily to sleep with one of the girls. Or at least that was the impression he gave, whatever the reality may have been. At one time I suspected that Catherine was his girl, but I have never been able to confirm that suspicion. When I asked the Filipino waiter, he replied in English, "Mr. Tom doesn't have a special girl. He's a really strange person: he takes photographs of the girls in different poses and gets up to some very naughty tricks that way. But that's all . . . There are some odd people in this world."

Now I'd seen enough of his high-handed, offensively wild behavior before that I wasn't particularly surprised; but his carryings-on on this particular night seemed excessive—it was more than his simply casting aside all reserve in the absence of any other customers. He must have had some deep inner anxiety. He must have felt unable to relax, as if he were constantly being pursued by someone. That was why he drank so much, and shouted, and danced so wildly—it was all in order to mask that anxiety. Come to think of it, when I entered the room a while before, Tomoda had been talking quietly with the girls. It was after catching sight of my face that he started to get restless and fidgety. Almost as if I had carried in with me something shadowy and extremely ominous to him . . .

"Tom! What happened?" This was accompanied by raucous laughter from Flora. "Tom! Tom, you old drunk!"

Tomoda, pushed away by Flora, fell on his rear end on the wooden floor of the hall.

He sat there with his legs spread and his belly pushed forward like a fat ceramic Billiken. The girls tried to raise him to his feet by taking hold of his hands and pulling mightily, but his belly was so big that it was hard going. They'd get him halfway up only for him to slip back and end up sitting on the floor again. Catherine got his hat and set it on his head. Rosa took off her bead necklace and hung it around his neck. Suddenly Tomoda folded his legs and assumed the expression of the Great Buddha. Then, just as suddenly, he got up, grabbed Flora again, and shouted, "Apache dance, apache dance!" Now, he knew how to tango, but Tomoda's apache dance was truly hit or miss. He would violently shove the woman away from him, hoist her into the air, grab her by the hips—it was as rough as any judo practice session. Flora's red hair—it must have been dyed: it was of an extraordinary redness—fell down over her forehead like flames, the seams of her dress came apart here and there, and at times her shoulders were bared. Both the man and the women there were drunk and thought nothing of the licentious scene. They gazed at it, chattering away in English or French: It had the feel of a bistro in Paris or some such city, not of Yokohama, Japan.

"Mr. K.! Mr. K.!" Tomoda grabbed my arm from behind, dazed as I was at the sight before me. "I'm drunk! Drunk as a skunk tonight, I am! And I like to really let loose at a time like this, so come on and dance along with me." He was talking English to me, and there was something strangely pushy in his manner, like a man pretending to be drunk so as to put pressure on someone else.

"Oh yeah? Are you interested in that one!" He moved his jaw in Edna's direction with a little sneer. "Well, what about her?"

"Not bad."

"You're impressed, aren't you?" Tomoda said with a loud laugh. "I wasn't telling you any lies! If you want her, go right ahead."

Edna had been sitting off by herself in a corner playing the guitar; but as the party got wilder, she put the instrument aside, as if resigned to not being heard, and folded her hands gracefully on her lap. Perhaps because she was a recent arrival not yet used to the place, she sat there quietly, her dark eyes gazing downward, and leaned against the back of her chair abstractedly. She was wearing Western clothes, but she had something of the erotic charm of a Japanese geisha. I looked again at the beautifully rounded lines of her shoulders. The hands resting on her lap were faintly white, like fine ivory, setting off the rosy color of her fingertips.

"I like her calm and gentle manner."

"If you like her, go on up to the second floor. You're going to spend the night here anyway, aren't you?"

"Hmm, I wonder. It's eleven already," I replied, taking my watch from my vest pocket.

"Oh, stay, stay! You can't be very busy just now."

"I don't mind staying, but that wasn't what I came for tonight."

"Why do you make such a big thing of it?" Tomoda gave another great laugh.

"Actually, I have something to tell you: I got a reply from Madam Matsunaga Shigeko."

I said this out of the blue, and then quickly added, "She says she's sure you're her husband. Your photos are very different, to be sure; but nonetheless, she says, her intuition tells her that Tomoda Ginzō is Matsunaga Gisuke."

"Hey, don't startle me like that! It's a bad joke you're making."

Tomoda looked as if he had swallowed a great lump of something or other, and was staring so hard at me that his eyes almost started from his head.

"No, that's what she wrote. And not only that: she asked me to describe your character in more detail."

"What a pushy dame! The photos are different, so that should settle the matter. Why does she carry on with her suspicions like this? She's being discourteous to you as well!"

"There's no point in getting so angry. Her husband has run off somewhere, and she's feeling desperate, so she imagines various possibilities."

"That's what I can't stand about novelists! You're too sympathetic when it comes to women."

"Well of course I sympathize with her. The calligraphy in her first letter was so refined, so unlike today's style—I fell in love with it. If I were her husband, the sight of that letter would make me want to go right back home to her."

"Why don't you, then? Go back in place of her husband."

"Listen, all joking aside, why don't you write her a letter yourself? Explain who you are, what kind of person, and convince her that you could not possibly be Matsunaga so-and-so. Perhaps you should include a copy of your family register, too."

"There's no need for me to do anything of the kind."

"You may feel no need to do so, but think of how she must feel."

"I have no sympathy for that woman."

"Well, but, if you leave things as they are, she'll be all the more suspicious of you. Doesn't that bother you?"

"No, it doesn't. I sent her the photograph, and that's the end of it. Let's stop talking about it."

"What a mess! The poor lady regards me as her only hope. I can't just abandon her; but I don't know enough about you to give a detailed explanation of your character, as she asks . . ." I played the innocent in saying this, but Tomoda glared at me as if I'd threatened him: "If you knew something, would you tell her?"

"Of course I would. In fact, I've already told her everything I do know."

"What sorts of things?"

"Everything I know. Our conversation of the other evening, our relationship, the matter of the ring—basically everything."

When I mentioned the ring, Tomoda could not repress a look of anger in his eyes.

He raised his hand, as if to strike me. Had we been alone, he might actually have done so, but he just made a disgusted sound and paced back and forth two or three times in irritation.

"That was very bad of you, to do such a thing! That's what's so awful about the Japanese! Drinking buddies are supposed to keep one another's secrets, you know."

"What are you two talking about in Japanese?" shouted Flora in a voice slurred with drink. "Shut up, shut up! Japanese is forbidden here!"

"Ah, but that was a slight infraction of the rules. I thought it would be far worse to lie to Shigeko. And besides, though it may make you even more angry to hear this, I feel Shigeko has her reasons for harboring suspicions about you."

"Oh, yeah? What might they be . . . ?" Tomoda had been pacing the floor, but now he stopped in his tracks, as if he'd been struck by a bullet.

"Think about it: you and I have been acquainted with one another for a very long time, yet every few years all contacts cease. And those periods exactly coincide with Matsunaga's return to his hometown. It was only when I read Shigeko's letter that I realized this; and I found it so strange that I wrote back to her about it—just my impressions, you know."

"So you . . ."

Just as Tomoda started to speak, there was a click, click, click: someone had made the lights in the room turn red, then blue, then pitch black.

"Oh, stop it, would you?" shrieked Catherine.

"Tom! Stop speaking in Japanese! We're all bored to tears."

"Tom can't hold his liquor. Why is he so mad at Mr. K. all of a sudden?"

"Don't worry. It's nothing. This novelist here is head over heels in love with some crazy woman, and I was just giving him some advice. That's the way it is, isn't it, Mr. K.?"

"Right. That's exactly the way things stand."

Tomoda went into a spasm of laughter. The clicks and dazzling changes in lighting continued, so I couldn't see the expression on his face . . .

PART 4

What became of Tomoda Ginzō?

I knew nothing about his whereabouts after that evening.

That was the last time he came to Number 27, and the place itself closed shortly thereafter. When he disappeared in 1915, Number 10, which had been his haunt, had soon become a vacant property as well.

So Tomoda's third period of disappearance had doubtless begun. I was not sure whether that had anything to do with Matsunaga Gisuke or not, however . . .

In October of the following year, 1921, I received word from Shigeko that Matsunaga Gisuke had returned to his hometown of Yagyumura, Soekami District, in Yamato. Once again he had returned in the fourth year of his disappearance. Shigeko's letter tells in detail of how happy the family was when he reappeared in front of his home after such a long absence, and of the scene of meeting between father and children, husband and wife; but I will leave all such details to the reader's imagination. I would add only that his eldest daughter, Taeko, who had so longed to see her father, was, by some happy chance, just recovering from her serious illness. Thus the Matsunaga family experienced a double degree of happiness.

Shigeko did not fail to report to me often on how Matsunaga behaved and what his days were like after he had settled down once again to life in the country. According to her account, her husband said not a word about where he had spent the past few years; but he had come back in Japanese dress carrying only a small satchel with him. That was on an evening in autumn: He was terribly tired and thin, but also very kind and gentle, even on the verge of tears, in his attitude toward the family—in short, everything was just as it had been on his previous return home. And not only that: Shigeko was able to ascertain shortly after his return that he had in his satchel all the things that had been there before—that postcard, those photographs, the personal seal, and the amethyst ring.

"Why does my husband still have such things? If I could have you look at them and tell me whether or not they are unquestionably Mr. Tomoda's possessions, my doubts could be cleared up, but . . . ," she wrote me at one point. "Now that my husband has come back, one might say that there is no need to pursue these suspicions of mine any further; but it is hard to tell if he might not leave home again in another three or four years, and so I feel I want to know the truth, once and for all, just in case. I sometimes quietly take out the photo of Mr. Tomoda that you kindly sent me and compare it with my husband's face. But Mr. Tomoda is young, and my husband old; the one is fat, and the other thin. And so it seems hard to accept that they are the same person. But then at other times I see some resemblance between their faces. And so I am left all adrift." There was no one else with whom she could share her suspicions, so she somehow found the time to make these appeals to me, it seemed.

The following year, at the end of March 1922, I traveled from Kyoto to Nara and stayed for a while at a hotel there. Shigeko learned of this from a newspaper and sent a letter to me at the hotel.

> I understand that you are staying for a while in Nara. Nara is only a little over twenty kilometers from here, and it would make me so happy if I could see you at some point during your stay. To reach Yagyumura, you would get off at Kasagi Station on the Kansai line; we are on the way to Tsukigase,

famous for its plum blossoms. Just now the plum blossoms are at their most beautiful, and if you happen to be going to Tsukigase, you would pass through our village. Might you not have time to stop for a while? I would be most grateful if you would visit our home and allow me to thank you for your kindnesses of the past two years. I would also like to introduce you to my husband and take advantage of your observation of him to resolve my long-standing suspicions. Let me assure you that, though my husband knows that you and I have been corresponding from time to time, he has never asked any intrusive questions. I have always told him that I am writing you out of admiration for your works, and he seems glad that, during his long absences, I have been able to relieve the lonely hours by reading your writings . . .

This letter of Shigeko's greatly aroused my curiosity. I decided to visit her home with the aim of seeing not the plum blossoms but the person and personality of Matsunaga Gisuke.

I left Nara at eight the next morning and got off the train at Kasagi, the third stop. Shared taxis for Tsukigase left from the front of the station. The sky was so beautiful that day, however, that it seemed a shame to go by car, and so I set off on foot along the pretty path to Yagyumura, some ten kilometers distant.

Numerous cars loaded with plum blossom viewers passed me on the way. They dirtied the clear country air, emitting ugly clouds of sooty exhaust as they went by; and I was immediately confirmed in my view that I had done well to walk. Only one who walks can understand the sweetness of strolling along a road in Yamato on such a fine spring day. The road I was on must have been the prefectural road that runs through Tsukigase to Ueno in Iga. Apart from the Yoshino area, Yamato has no steep mountains or dark, secluded valleys. Flat, faintly yellow roads pass through villages scattered here and there, crossing small streams, and winding along numerous hills. It seems at first glance a very ordinary kind of scenery, but these everyday, just-as-you-find-them fields and paddies are so peaceful and spring-like! And how beautiful is everything that lies spread out before you: distant storehouse walls, thatched roofs, trees along the roads, rice paddies, stands of bamboo.

All these perfectly ordinary things gleam in the sunlight, intoxicating the viewer. I was wearing a winter coat, and as I let my feet take me forward at a natural pace, the inside of my shirt became damp with perspiration. When from time to time I stopped and gazed at the view, I could see red mist trailing gracefully over the foot of a mountain far in the distance; small birds twittered ceaselessly in the sky above me, and I seemed to find myself in "A Peaceful Village," as depicted in some painting. I imagine that the legendary "Peach Stream of Wu Ling" must have been an idealization of just such a calm and peaceful atmosphere. The fields of tea plants that covered the slopes around me especially delighted my eyes. They formed feminine-looking hillocks, with a gentle roundedness; and the tea plants on the sides of those hillocks seemed like balls of velvet aglow in the golden sunlight—pure magic! I forgot entirely why I had come this way. I felt I would never tire of walking along this road, no matter how long the day.

Yagyumura itself is a rather large village, and I had to walk quite far after entering it. But I had been told that the Matsunaga house was one of the oldest and grandest in the village, and I soon found it. There was no need for me send in my card: Shigeko had been standing in the inner garden and at once came to the gate to welcome me. Right behind her trotted a little girl of four or five who turned out to be Fumiko, her second daughter, born in 1919.

"It was such a fine day today that I thought you might be coming . . . ," Shigeko said. Her looks were as in the photograph, but her cheeks were a bit red, perhaps due to the sunlight. Her old-fashioned, married woman's coiffure was ample, and she looked two or three years younger than her actual age of thirty-five. She spoke in a clear way, and her kimono of ordinary *meisen* silk was not unbecoming.

The house was that of a wealthy peasant of the Edo period, quite unchanged, and the rooms inside were dim. I had been shown to the guest parlor toward the rear of the house and had time for a relaxed conversation with Shigeko as we waited for her husband to come and formally welcome me. I began by asking about her splendid calligraphy, since I had a keen interest in it. She told me that she had graduated from a girls' school in Nara, and that was her only formal education; but since marrying into the Matsunaga family, she had read literature and practiced calligraphy whenever she had time. I also learned from our conversation that the Matsunagas were descendants of Matsunaga Hisahide of the sixteenth-century Warring States period and had lived in this area for hundreds of years. Learning to write in the ancient style was not so much a result of her own tastes as it was of the customs of the Matsunaga household. Her husband had at first hated his family's outmoded ways, right up to the death of his mother. Even after her passing, the old customs were still observed; and it had occurred to Shigeko that her husband's departures and disappearances might have been due to that fact. But for the past ten years and more, as his temperament grew gentler, his tastes had also gradually changed. Now he was delighted that she studied *waka* poetry and read classical literature; and he urged her each morning, almost as one of her daily tasks, to "practice your calligraphy with this," handing her "The Universal Gate Chapter" of the *Lotus Sutra*. And he himself would bring from the storehouse various works in classical Chinese that his grandfather had collected in his day and delve into them.

Since our conversation had shifted to her husband, I asked about his health.

"He's getting better little by little, but it's not a rapid recovery, so he says the three of us should go to the thirty-three holy places again this spring. Last time he made a complete recovery by doing so," Shigeko answered.

Shigeko said that Gisuke's weight was only a little over ninety pounds. His stomach had always been weak, and so he had little appetite, eating only the equivalent of one meal a day and drinking hardly any sake. On the other hand, he seemed to be taking care of himself and doing his best to preserve his health.

Thus, though he was sickly, he had never suffered a serious illness. People of this type often seemed to have good longevity, and so Shigeko was not too worried on that score. Their eldest daughter, Taeko, had been getting more and more healthy lately and had been sent to live with relatives in Nara, where she could attend a school for girls.

As she recounted in detail these recent happenings in response to my questions, she seemed much more cheerful than I had imagined from her letters; indeed, she appeared to be a fortunate wife and mother. If only her husband would settle down permanently and not go off again as he had done, Shigeko, living in this lovely and peaceful village, would no doubt spend the rest of her life in a state as calm and happy as this day had been. Even when my questions touched on the matter of the satchel, her face remained more untroubled than I had expected. She explained that she would like to show the satchel to me, but with her husband there in the house it would not do to bring it out. She went on to describe in detail the shape and look of the satchel, the design of the amethyst ring, and the like. Since I have not seen the things themselves, I cannot say for sure; but from what she said, they seemed to tally perfectly with Tomoda Ginzō's possessions.

As the two of us talked, uncertain footsteps, like those of an invalid, sounded heavily from the corridor, and soon Matsunaga Gisuke himself entered the room. Gisuke looked embarrassed as our eyes met. He was supposed to be only forty-two, but he had the look of an elderly man close to fifty. There was a network of fine wrinkles on his forehead and neck, his hair was reddish-brown, and his sideburns were white. When he spoke, his prominent Adam's apple moved painfully—or, rather, every joint in his scraggly body, which reminded me of a withered tree on which a kimono had been hung, seemed to creak with pain. I thought of a puppet whose strings had become tangled: they might at any moment break and his whole body collapse in a heap.

Gisuke himself must have been assailed by such a fear. The way he held himself and moved about was oddly cautious; he seemed to be taking great care of his body, as if it were a fragile piece of porcelain. When he sat kneeling in formal style, he made sure to keep one hand on the tatami to support his feeble torso. If he failed to do so, he appeared to get dizzy and looked as if he might fall backward. "A very severe case of neurasthenia," I thought to myself.

When, earlier, I had seen the photograph of him on pilgrimage, I had noticed how sharp his gaze was—pathologically sharp. And indeed he did have the eyes of someone who is extremely misanthropic, of someone atremble with paranoia. His pallid, yellowish face with its sparse whiskers and harsh expression, the hoarse voice in which he grudgingly made his few comments, his tobacco-stained teeth—it goes without saying that none of these reminded me in the least of Tomoda. Realizing from his manner how unbearable it was for him that we should be together like this, I decided to take my leave in good time.

"He's not like that with the family, and sometimes even talks a bit himself when he's in the mood—you yourself, sir, come up in our conversations from time to time. But when he's in the presence of a stranger, well, you see how he is. Please forgive us," said Shigeko as she saw me off at the gate.

"Oh no, there's nothing to apologize for. Only, Madam, I must say that your husband is certainly not Tomoda Ginzō. You said that they resembled each other, but that must have been due to your great anxiety. Your husband really does seem quite ill, so please do take best care of him." I said this as I took my leave, observing a trace of sadness on Shigeko's face. She remained standing at the gate, gazing after me for some time.

Then, seduced by the fine weather, I went on to Tsukigase. On the way back, I visited Ueno in Iga, where I saw the well-known "lock-maker's crossroad," associated with the revenge attack of the Edo period swordsman Araki Mataemon, and then paid my respects at the tomb of the haiku poet Bashō. The town of Ueno was small but pleasant. That evening I enjoyed looking at the dwarf plum trees at the Daiseirō Inn and spent the night there.

PART 5

(Tomoda Ginzō's confession)

. . . . Mr. K, as a novelist you must know all sorts of strange facts and unusual stories. But how to get you truly to understand my strange situation? I don't know where to begin. Even if you listen carefully to everything I have to say, you may not find it easy to believe me.

(Having said this, Tomoda Ginzō downed another glass of cognac. It was in June of this year, 1925, and I had not seen Tomoda for quite a while when we met at the Café Sans Souci in Kobe for the first time.)

I was born in Yagyumura, Soekami District, Yamato. Ours was an old, established family, descended from Matsunaga Hisahide of the Warring States period. So my officially registered name is Matsunaga Gisuke. What? You want to know who the other Matsunaga Gisuke, whom you met in March of the year before last, was? Well, just wait a bit. It'll all become clear as I tell my story.

In 1905, when I was twenty-five, I married a woman named Shigeko. Let me make it clear that I was not in love with Shigeko— not at all. I was just out of university and didn't want to get married; but with my father dead, I was the head of the family, and I couldn't ignore family needs and amuse myself as I wished, precisely because we were such an old family. On my mother's orders, I unwillingly came back from Tokyo and took Shigeko as my wife. Of course I was unhappy about it: It was unbearable to think of wasting my whole life deep in the country. I was young, after all, and full of vitality, and I couldn't endure a life without stimulation. And I am by nature a hedonist, and lazy, and hate having to work at anything. Fortunately or unfortunately, I had enough to live on without working, and I dreamed of pursuing pleasure whenever I could. I longed for the city. I couldn't go as far as Tokyo, but I managed by hook or by crook to find business that would take me to Kyoto or Osaka from time to time, where I spent my money in the pleasure quarters of Gion and Shinmachi. I got tired of the world of the geishas, however, and was always looking for new pleasures. At the time, nothing else was available to me, and I was feeling rather desperate. But then, before long, my mother died, and that one great obstacle was gone. There might still be carping relatives, but now there was no one I was afraid of. Well, I could hardly control the itch to be off. Now I was free to go anywhere I pleased! And if I found a foreign land that was to my taste, I wouldn't have to come back to Japan at all! And so at last I decided to go to Paris, which I had been so eager to see for so long . . .

As you know, although I am Japanese, I virtually lead the life of a Westerner. My tastes in liquor and women constitute almost the whole of my life, and I detest Japanese sake and Japanese women. I am a complete and extreme worshipper of the West. I suppose that I developed this tendency out of a reaction against my upbringing in an established provincial family, hedged about with old customs. And then, while I was living in Tokyo, a dissolute friend's introduction allowed me once or twice to have a peek at a strange, dreamlike world in Yokohama, one that Japanese are rarely allowed to enter: the white man's realm of pleasure.

At any rate, from then on I cursed every aspect of Oriental taste. Just as the interior of the family house in Yagyumura was dim and gloomy, so all aspects of Eastern taste were gloomy. "Elegance" and "refinement" were the complete of opposite of bright openness and frankness. They were not for healthy persons, young persons, persons with a proper degree of vitality. Doddering old men were forced to find value and pleasure in such boring things. It was no more than an aesthetics of cranky resignation and mean-spirited pretense. Even in tasting the same pleasures as a Westerner, the Oriental stops at 50 or 60 percent and calls that "discreet good taste" or "refined beauty." But it's got nothing to do with "discreet good taste" or anything of the sort: Orientals simply lack the physical vitality to absorb as much as they would wish of the sensual stimuli available—in short, they don't have what it takes. So, for example, when it comes to singing, they don't open up their throats and let the sound emerge naturally; they sing in a constrained and unnatural voice and call that "chic." And when women appear before men, they don't try to show as much of their physical beauty as possible; instead, they hide it as much as they can under long sleeves and stiff obi sashes and claim that that is more "subtly erotic." In fact, though, that's not the case. When they sing, they can't manage the high notes and use falsetto instead, and they quickly run out of breath; and as for displaying their natural beauty, if they try to do so in an obvious way, they reveal the muddiness of their complexions and the unattractive lines of their arms and legs. In short, again, they don't have what it takes. Since they can't do anything about that, they try to fool the world with words like "chic" and "subtly erotic."

So it seemed to me, and therefore I despised Oriental taste. The yellowish color of Eastern complexions struck me as unpleasant. My only real sorrow was that I, too, had such a face. Whenever I looked in the mirror, I felt how unfortunate I was to have been born in one of the "yellow countries." And I felt that the longer I stayed in a "yellow country," the yellower my own complexion would become. My wish was to leave this lukewarm, depressing, gloomy land as quickly as possible and escape to the West. There, in place of such *warped tastes as "chic" and "the patina of age," one had full-voiced music that sang brilliantly of pleasure. There one could find bodies that became all the more beautiful as they were openly exposed. The reverse of "discreet good taste," the reverse of "implication"—strong colors, extreme stimuli, alcohol that inflames the tongue, a positive hedonism that tastes pleasures well beyond the limit, an intoxicating world of which one would never tire—all were there! It was Paris that I was aiming for, as the quintessential West.*

I left in the summer of 1916, when Shigeko was pregnant. I was resolved in my own mind not to return to Japan while I had breath, and I made arrangements to ensure that my family would not be placed in a difficult situation afterward. I believe that Shigeko had some intimations of my decision as well. Inwardly, she knew how selfish her husband was and could do nothing except take whatever I said with good grace. I felt a touch of sadness when I left my hometown, but no sooner was I onboard ship than such things were completely forgotten. The reason was that, even before landing in France, I could make a beginning in my new life of pleasure soon after leaving Japan, in Shanghai! To be honest, in all the ports I passed through at that time, I became infatuated with women who lived there. Forget about Paris and spend your life here, with this woman, I thought, wherever I happened to be. But then, when I reached the next port, a new and as yet untried world would welcome me. The further away from Japan I moved, the deeper grew my dissipation, the stronger my intoxication. Thus, when I reached Paris, my life of decadence reached its peak.

It is almost impossible for the modest minds of Orientals to conceive of the dazzling, dissipated, sick, and strange things that Paris holds—a whirlpool of lust of every possible mode and kind—it makes one dizzy. The Paris that I now saw was like the one that I had barely glimpsed in my dreams—a land of lewd pleasures that I thought could never actually exist in this world. And I, of course, was willing to cast aside body and soul to be swept into this whirlpool. The lover of pleasure accepts the fact that he will be sacrificed to pleasure. The poison of liquor, the poison of tobacco, the poison of rich foods, the poison of women—if on account of these poisons, his body exhausts itself and dies, why, that is precisely what he wants. I myself felt, each time I indulged in pleasure, that this might be the last time. Will I die today or tomorrow? I wondered as I gave myself over to pleasure. This "premonition of death" did not make a coward of me, however; on the contrary, it allowed me to plunge with more courage into the pit of hell. Precisely because I was aware of "death," wine and women bewitched me all the more.

By the time a year and a half had passed since my arrival in Paris, I had assimilated myself completely, both psychologically and physically, to "the West." Now everyone who travels in the West takes on certain Western traits, but I daresay there are few who have been transformed, even on a physiological level, as thoroughly as I was, or in so short a period. I myself didn't realize I had undergone so extreme a change; but when, by chance, I came across a Japanese in the street around that time, not even one of them recognized me as a fellow countryman. Some said I was an Italian, some a Spaniard. And I myself was amazed at my own transformation when one evening I took a woman friend to a café and found a Japanese seated at the next table. Looking at him, I recognized my old friend S., with whom I had been on close terms when we were at university. Yet even when he looked right at me, S. showed no sign of recognition. I thought it very odd, but when I realized that I had changed so much that even S. did not know it was me, I also felt pleased beyond words. I went so far as to stand up, bend over so that my face was closer to S.'s, and address him in French; but even hearing my voice, S. did not recognize me. I was so happy that I rushed back to my rooms and stared at myself in the mirror. Then, remembering that I had a photograph that had been taken in Japan at the time of my departure, I found it and compared the two images. My, what a surprise! Face, physique, skin color, the expression in the eyes—was it possible for a human being to change this much in the space of only a year and a half, even given a change in his environment? I had been thin when I was in my hometown, but during the voyage I had drunk liquor every day and every night, and began to put on weight as a result. By the time I reached France, I could no longer wear my old clothing, so I realized that I was putting on weight at a fast pace; but I didn't notice until then, when I compared my present self with the photograph, that my weight gain was so great that my whole image had been transformed. Looking at the photo of myself as I had been, I felt not so much that I had changed as that, without my knowing it, I had become an entirely different person! The Matsunaga Gisuke who had been born in Yagyumura, Soekami District, in the province of Yamato as the descendant of Matsunaga Hisahide, had at some point ceased to be present in this world, and in his place was this man—a Japanese, an Italian, a Spaniard?, one whose very race and nationality were unclear—standing before the mirror. And this was my present "self." When I realized that, I felt—how shall I put it?—something like a strange sort of terror. In Western tales of the mysterious, it often happens that a human being exactly like oneself makes an appearance; but my experience was the exact opposite: I myself had turned into another person. I felt as if I were possessed by some devil. "Was I really this person until a year and a half ago?" I thought, as I stared intently at the photo of "Matsunaga Gisuke" once again. Of course—it was only natural that S. did not recognize me now because, looking at this, even I could not conceive that it was a photo of myself!

That's right—I'm not Matsunaga Gisuke anymore. The Japanese in this photograph, whom I don't recognize—this scrawny, gloomy-looking Oriental—has nothing to do with me! That's what I shouted within myself as I threw the photograph to the floor. A new kind of joy welled up inside me then. I was no longer a Japanese. I was a perfect Westerner. At that thought, I started to sing a song of victory and, raising both hands in the air, danced wildly about. Japanese foods, Japanese dress, all sorts of Japanese customs came to mind; but I recalled them, not as past experiences of my own, but

as elements in the daily life of an as yet uncivilized Oriental race. If
one embarked from Marseilles here in France and sailed eastward,
eastward for a month and a half, one would come at last to the
island nation of Japan. Its inhabitants had yellow faces and lived in
dimly lit houses. When they spoke, they mumbled in low voices, not
opening their mouths properly. In the morning, they drank bean-
paste soup from wooden bowls painted with black lacquer. What a
colorless, gloomy sort of life they led! And they had no beds or chairs:
when they were up, they sat with legs crossed or folded under them
in low-ceilinged rooms. Just to imagine how cramped it all is makes
me choke! If my present self, who was not Matsunaga Gisuke—at
the time I called myself by a French name, "Jacques Moran"—if I
were to be set down in the midst of such a life, I was sure I could
not survive a single day. But I imagine you will want to ask me why
I am now living in Japan, why I did not stay in the West for the
rest of my life. Ah, yes, that's the point: here, too, I sense the devils
using me for their sport. As I just explained, I had become a devotee
of Paris, and I piled indulgence upon indulgence day after day. Of
course I had no intention of returning to Japan, alive or dead. I had
got fatter and fatter recently: when I was at my heaviest, I weighed
around 170 pounds. My complexion became all the whiter, and my
cheeks were a radiant, rosy red. "Alive or dead" I said, but death was
the furthest thing from my mind at the time, so I drained the wine
of pleasure to the very bottom of the cup. No matter how much I
drank, I never had enough. If a man wants to live in good health, he
should live in the Western way—strongly, optimistically, actively.
Whether it's food or sex, he should feast to his heart's content until
his stomach is well and truly full. Oriental-style passivity makes
people weak and sickly. Look at me! Since assimilating to the West,
see how strong and healthy I've become! No matter how I indulge
myself, no matter how I ignore the traditional Eastern rules of
health, I just grow ever more stout. This sturdy frame of mine is the
best evidence for the victory of activism over passivity. I gradually
came to believe all this and grew more venturesome as a result. My

life at the time was so amusing: the climate was good, the food was delicious, I had no worries, I was successful in numerous romantic adventures, and when I gambled I always won. I was sailing with a fine wind at my back as I made my way smoothly across an endless sea of "happiness." I still had plenty of money with me, and even if it ran out, there were lots of ways to make a living if one were not too choosy about what one did. Why, even darkies from Africa were able to act the clown and live well enough in Paris. I certainly could do the same if need be. And if worse came to worst, I would die like a dog by the roadside.

That was how carefree I was feeling when suddenly they came upon me—those devils' tricks that I mentioned earlier. It was on an afternoon of fine weather—what we'd call in Japan "a bright Indian summer day"—and I was strolling along a boulevard. The line of trees was so beautiful that I stopped and gazed up at the blue, blue sky that showed through the leaves of one of the tall plane trees. At that moment, somehow I felt dizzy, and the whole sky seemed to fill with minuscule bubbles. Suddenly everything went black, and I began to fall backward. It was just a momentary attack, and I recovered almost before I had time to think "How strange!" I forgot all about it that day; but from then on, such attacks would occur from time to time. If I looked up suddenly, I felt dizzy. I had a dull, heavy feeling, as if a weight were suspended from the back of my head; it was as if I were being pulled backward. Gradually, however, to my great surprise, the attacks started to come not only when I looked up but also when I bent down. Once, when I had dropped a glove on the street and stooped to pick it up, all the blood in my body seemed to rush to my brain, the veins in my neck swelled as if they were about to burst, and my face grew hot and red as a boiled octopus. I felt faint and was about to fall forward to the ground. 'Oh, God, this is strange. What's happening to me?" I felt a bit panicky. But even perfectly healthy people occasionally experience vertigo for some reason or other, so I told myself it probably wasn't anything to worry about, just a passing phenomenon. However, it began to happen whenever I leaned forward to tie my shoelaces or wash my hair, for example. The most extreme example was one day when I was having a bowl of hot soup at a restaurant. The blood rushed suddenly to my head, I felt faint, and I nearly did a bow into the soup bowl. The tip of my nose was almost touching the soup when I managed to recover myself—but what a surprise that was! Perhaps it was partly because the soup was too hot; but if just leaning forward to eat it could do this to me, how could I go out in public? Was I suffering from neurasthenia? Or from some vile disease that was attacking my brain? It was all too mysterious; and now, suddenly, I began to lose my nerve. I tried to tell myself that even now "I could die like a dog by the roadside, if it came to that"; but even slight vertigo or a rush of blood to the head caused my heart to pound wildly and plunged me into unbearable fear. Panic attacks eat into a man's soul and mount assaults impossible to resist. So even if you are prepared to die, you can't prevent them. The feeling "I don't care if I die" and "a terror of death" can coexist. You don't care if you die, but what is frightening remains frightening. When panic sets in, the slightest things can be terrifying. "You stupid bastard! You said you didn't care if you died, and now you're scared of something like this?" But even as I was telling myself that, my whole body trembled and my face took on an ashen color. I fell into a cold sweat and seemed about to collapse. When this happened without warning in the middle of the street or among a crowd of strangers, I would start to run for all I was worth, like some madman. I would scratch at and pull out my hair. If I was at home, I would kick at the floorboards, butt my head against the doors and walls, toss about anything and everything that was to hand, and finally rush to the bathroom sink and pour water over my head. My pulse would speed up more and more until it seemed as if my heart would burst from its violent thumping. My terror would last only about five or ten minutes: if I drank two or three glasses of brandy, it would usually quiet down. But I never knew when an attack would come, so I lived each day in fear. And I kept my bottle of brandy with me at all times.

These ridiculous panic attacks at first occurred only when I was on my own, so no one noticed them except me, and they were easy to deal with. But then, bit by bit, they began to occur in company. I was at the time in love with a dancing girl named Susanne and saw her constantly. Then one night we met at our usual place, as arranged, and I was sitting on a bench, exchanging sweet nothings with her. Now Susanne had exceptionally white skin, and I was staring at her pale white arms, there right before my eyes, as if struck anew at their beauty. "Oh, what splendid skin she has!" I said to myself, as always; but that night I gazed at her with a special feeling of enchantment. And as long as I focused on her arms, I was in a kind of trance, as if my very soul had been spirited off; but then my gaze shifted, and I looked at the white flesh of her shoulders, even more strikingly white than her arms. At that moment, I shivered, as if my hair were standing on end. The instant my optical nerve was exposed to the extraordinary whiteness of the skin of that shoulder, I felt dizzy, and something cold seemed to press against my chest. The feelings "Ah, how white it is!" and "How beautiful!" turned all at once into a kind of terror. My legs began to tremble as if I were peering into a deep valley from atop a high, steep cliff. To feel terror at the sight of a woman's pure white skin may seem ludicrous, but if the skin is extraordinarily beautiful, and if it is part of the body of the woman you're infatuated with, wouldn't anyone feel a kind of chill in his heart? Well, that stimulus or shock was intense in my case.

"Oh, what's wrong with you? Your face is dead white!" said Susanne, drawing close to me in a concerned way; but that meant that her white skin appeared all the more threatening, and my terror reached its peak. I pushed Susanne's hand aside with all my might, rushed to the sink, and splashed water over my head. I remember shouting, "Susanne, Susanne, quickly, give me some brandy . . . ," and then I faded out . . .

"Oh, what an unhappy wretch I am! To have a pretty girl like that at hand yet lack the energy to enjoy making love to her!" That's *what I thought as I returned to my lodgings, fleeing from Susanne's embrace and pitying myself as I did so. My immediate concern was how to get out of my promise to meet Susanne again the very next evening. Rather than lose her affection by making an ugly spectacle of myself as I had the previous night, would it not be better to cast her aside myself? Not that I was tired of Susanne or anything of the sort. When I thought of her waiting for me again that night, my desire to see her was unbearably strong. Once the panic attack was over, even the pure white color of her skin became not terrifying but the seed of unforgettable fascination; and I asked myself how I could ever throw aside a woman like her, as my love for her deepened. And in the end I would go to her, praying in my heart, "May an attack like that not be visited upon me again tonight!" And so we continued to meet, with attacks, massive or moderate, occurring on most evenings. Worst of all was the fact that it was not only the whiteness of her skin but any excessively strong stimulus from something beautiful or pleasurable that did me in. If I forgot myself and tried to scale the peaks of love's pleasures, the valley of terror would immediately open before me and I would be dragged down to the cold depths of the earth. When her burning lips came close, when our arms were entwined as if never to be separated, when we flirted with each other, uttering innocent, excited cries—at such times the attacks would make a point of coming to spoil our pleasure. When the pleasure was especially intense, the terror, too, would be all the more intense, as if to smash our pleasure to smithereens. Consequently, even if an attack did not start, I would be threatened by premonitions of terror and be unable to give myself fully to pleasure. How ironic it was: I, who believed in a positively hedonistic sort of life that sought to take pleasure to its natural limits and beyond, was now in a position in which I was unable to put my creed into practice . . .*

. . . This is what I want you to hear, Mr. K.: After I'd fallen into this miserable situation, can you imagine how much I agonized over it day after day? The skies of Paris were as bright a blue as ever; the

sun shone with the same gentle radiance; countless beautiful women passed along the streets. Yet if I looked up into the sky, I became dizzy; if exposed to the sunlight, I felt faint; and if I saw a woman's white skin, I was afraid. None of these things was any consolation to me. My vision was now so weak that I could not even endure the rays of the sun. I shut myself up in a dim room away from the sunlight and lay perfectly still, like some kind of mole, brooding.

Then suddenly there came to my mind my ancestral home in Yamato—dim, like the room I was in now, but with a certain gentleness and softness about it. Only a year or two had passed since I abandoned that home, but it came back to me now like an old, old, distant memory of days gone by. For over two decades after I came into this world, I had lived in that house in accordance with the old ways: I remembered how at bedtime an old-fashioned paper lantern was lit, and how its faint, dreamlike glow spread softly over my pillow; I remembered the wooden ceiling and main pillar of the room, blackened with soot from the oil-lamps, and my wife's face as she drifted off under the counterpane, in the uncertain, flickering light . . .

"Oh, you mustn't think about Japan," I told myself, denying those thoughts over and over; but the more I denied them, the more those scenes revived within my memory with an inexpressible nostalgia. And it was not only thoughts of my hometown. I remembered also the pleasure districts of Gion and Shinmachi and the mysterious, understated sounds of the samisen and the restrained, well-practiced sound of the geishas' voices there. These things, which I had earlier rejected as catering to cranky resignation and mean-spirited pretense, now, strangely enough, brought, even in imagination, a sense of peace to my jangled nerves. And as for the color of a woman's skin—a yellowish hue seemed softer, sweeter, more deeply soothing to me from the heart than a starkly white one. Then I recalled the fragrance of the miso soup served each morning. The pickled vegetables, white rice, clear soup made with kelp stock, sea bream sashimi—the calm, settled harmony of colors when *these are set together on a lacquer serving tray, and the rich feel on one's tongue as they are eaten or drunk—I thought of them all. I rebuked myself: "So you're missing Japan now, are you? You damn fool! You coward!" But once those feelings start up in one, there's nothing to be done. Everything I saw and heard was compared to "oriental tastes," and things Western seemed merely flashy, showy, and shallow. Try as I might to ignore it, a voice was constantly whispering in my ear. "You're an Oriental, after all. No matter how intoxicated by the West you may be, you can never become a Westerner," it would urge. Wherever I went, the voice followed. At each of my three daily meals, the voice whispered, "How about it? Do you really find your food and drink delicious when you eat with this shiny metal cutlery and drink from these sparkling glasses? And what about this tablecloth and these porcelain plates? They're clean and sanitary, to be sure, but do they have any quiet elegance, any depth? Wouldn't eating from a lacquer bowl with lacquer chopsticks make things go down better? Don't you find eating with a knife and fork to be savage? Don't you think it a way of eating that is more bestial than human?" In this way, the voice tempted me.*

If I went to the opera, I heard a mean-spirited mocking whisper: "Hey—you can pretend that you love the Westerners' songs and drama, but it won't wash. You can't fool me! Just listen to the way that soprano and baritone are singing. They can sing loud and hit the high notes all right, but they sound like animals howling. See? When they sing at full volume, it makes your ears ring, as if your eardrums were about to burst. What you long for are the gentle songs sung in restrained tones by the people of your native place. Right? That's what you really want, isn't it?" The whispers grew gradually louder and more frequent until in the end I could hear them very clearly: "I'm giving you good advice: Go back to Japan! When you see too much of pure white things, or bright things, you get frightened—it's in your blood as an Oriental. If he lives in the midst of all this gaudy color, an Oriental is sure to become neurasthenic. No matter how hard you try to love a white woman, your very blood won't let you!"

I resisted this voice, but the terror I felt grew day by day, and I could do nothing about it. In the end, I felt anxious about all aspects of Western life—they made me shudder. When I walked alongside a tall building, when I used an elevator, when I drove in a car at high speed, when I stepped on hard, creaking floorboards or on sidewalks, when I was in a room surrounded on all four sides by walls on which there was no trace of the grain of natural wood—and when I smelt each and every odor, whether of face powder or perfume or clothing or food—the characteristic odor of the Caucasian race that permeated all these things began to disgust and nauseate me. "Come on now—you can't go on with things as they are. You can neither live nor die in this country. Get onboard some ship and leave these shores, even if only for a little while. Then you'll feel so relieved— your palpitations and your nerves will settle right down. Anyway, just try it, even if you think it won't work." Someone was tugging at my sleeve. The idea of returning to Japan was very distasteful, but there was something that kept driving me on from behind: "Run away! Hurry! Run away!" I rushed to get on a mail steamer and found myself gazing from its deck at the ever-retreating port of Marseilles, feeling both relief at being free and an intense regret that seemed to pull me back . . .

I daresay you remember, Mr. K., how we met for the first time at Kōnosu, "The Wild Goose's Nest," in Koami-chō—it must have been toward the end of 1908. Actually, I had just arrived back in Japan. Having disembarked in Kobe, I came straight to Tokyo without getting in touch with my relatives in Yamato. I still had some deep resistance to "oriental tastes," and the idea of beating a retreat to my native place seemed hateful to me. In Tokyo I ran into two or three acquaintances, none of whom recognized me as Matsunaga Gisuke, so I decided to retire for a while to some hot springs resort, regain my health, effect a complete cure of my neurasthenia, and then make my way back to the West somehow. Then when I met you, I used the false name "Tomoda Ginzō" for the first time. But my health did not improve at all after that; in fact, it grew worse and worse. I had little appetite, my sexual desire began to fail me, and I couldn't drink a drop of alcohol. Even the brandy that I had used as a kind of stimulant now simply increased my terror whenever I drank it. From the end of that year until the autumn of the next, I moved about from one hot springs to another: now Hakone, now Ikaho, now Beppu. At last I secluded myself in an inn at a hot springs deep in the mountains of Nagano, a place known to hardly anyone, where my life was like that of a Zen monk, far from all strong stimuli. Yet even that brought no improvement. My body grew weak and emaciated, and I didn't have the strength to walk. When I climbed up or came down the stairs, I staggered. "Oh, at this rate I may die soon. I wonder how the people back home are doing? Maybe if I went back and received my wife's tender care, I might get better," I would think, as the tears began to flow. I recalled how my wife had wept bitterly on the evening I left some four years before. Oh yes—she had been pregnant at the time. If the child was born and had grown up safe and sound, it would be in its fourth year by then, by traditional Japanese count . . . Then, oddly enough, I could hear an innocent child's voice calling "Daddy, Daddy!" as it stretched out its arms to me. And I could hear the voice of my wife, too, as she dandled the child in her arms: "Yes, yes, it's all right— don't cry, my sweet. Daddy's coming home . . ." As the longing for my home filled every corner of my being, my body grew weaker and weaker, so that I came to spend the whole day wrapped in the bed quilts, like some invalid unable to get up. Then one day, wondering how much thinner I might have become, I picked up the hand mirror that lay at my bedside and discovered that my face, with its starkly protruding cheekbones and bushy whiskers, had become—in general impression, complexion, look about the eyes, in fact everything— that of Matsunaga Gisuke once more.

My amazement at this change was twice as great as what I had experienced in the Parisian hotel. It felt weird. Jacques Moran, the man who might have been Japanese, Italian, or Spanish, whose race and nationality were unknown—and the man who introduced

himself as "Tomoda Ginzō" when you first met him some time
later—I was certainly "that man" until last year. But if he had
become "Matsunaga Gisuke" again, without his really knowing it,
then who in fact was I? Which was the real "I"? Had anyone else
apart from me ever had the strange experience of turning into a
completely different person in one year?

(Tomoda Ginzō seemed to be guided by some invisible power as
he said all this at one go. Now he leaned even further forward
and continued speaking.)

But this wasn't the only strange thing. I returned home,
intending to spend my whole life as a benevolent husband and
father and planning to be buried at the end in the soil of my native
place. My life during that period was as described by Shigeko in
her letters to you: from the autumn of 1909 to the spring of 1912,
I lived in my home in Yagyumura as a kind of rural sage. It was a
solitary, gloomy, monotonous kind of life, but precisely that solitude
and monotony calmed my nerves and relieved my anxiety. There are
various temples and other well-known sites in our neighborhood
that can provide peace to a troubled mind. In March the plum trees
bloom in Tsukigase; in April, the cherry trees of Yoshino blossom; in
May, there are the wisteria in Nara, and the young grass appears. I
take my wife and daughter and explore spring's beauties along the
roads of Yamato, visiting Nan'endō, Tōdaiji, Yakushiji, and Hōryūji.
When the three of us stand with hands folded in prayer before the
buddha images in the ancient temple chapels, a sense of joy at being
an Oriental wells up from deep within me. My father and mother
had no doubt come to this chapel and worshipped the image here.
Here, where we three, parents and child, were kneeling, generations
of our ancestors had prostrated themselves. When, imagining this, I
gazed up at the buddha images, I felt as if distant generations of our
ancestors were watching over us, and tears came to my eyes.
Thus, it seemed that I would spend the rest of my days

peacefully, without anxiety; but when those two and a half years
had passed, another change came upon me, completely unexpected
even by myself. At my weakest, my body weight had been only about
ninety pounds; but gradually I began to gain weight—although
looking at me, you couldn't tell—until I was about one hundred
pounds. Then, bit by bit, my tastes in food began to change. We
were a country household, so naturally we did not eat meat and
hardly ever ate raw fish. Our meals consisted of miso soup, pickles,
fresh vegetables and fruits. Now, when I first came back home, I
relished such simple, austere foods, but my tastes gradually began to
demand oily things, things with stronger flavors. "I won't last long
eating only food like this!" I would sometimes sigh, seated before my
dining tray and remembering the flavor of the chateaubriand and
the fragrance of the bouillabaisse I had enjoyed in Paris. I wanted
to eat something that would fill my stomach to the bursting point,
something that would set my tongue on fire, something that would
make the blood throughout my body seethe. Gluttony is a fearful
thing; if its desires are not satisfied, one's entire life begins to totter.
Greedy to eat, I would go off to Nara and Osaka determined to fill
myself full of nourishment of whatever kind: terrapin, eel, beef
sukiyaki—I ate such things to my heart's content. Next I tried the
taste of the alcohol that I had given up for so long. When I went
to a certain restaurant in Osaka and first broke my private rule
of temperance, I feared that the neurasthenia I had suffered from
might revive. And so I was a bit uneasy. But when I had my first
drink, everything was fine! I could look up, I could look down, I
could spin around, I could run off—no dizziness, no rush of blood
to my head. Riding an elevator was a pleasure. Racing along in an
automobile was a pleasure. Forgetting myself, I shouted out loud,
"I'm healthy! I'm free! Those hateful panic attacks have packed
themselves off somewhere!" Intense sexual desire, a heart that
longs for limitless pleasure—these pushed their way through my
drunkenness.

Having said this much, I'm sure I don't have to explain why I left home for the second time in the summer of that year. For the same reasons as before, my native place became distasteful to me, Japan became distasteful, the Orient became distasteful, and passivity became distasteful. Once again I longed for Susanne's white skin, I yearned after the gay, colorful nights of Montmartre, and I wished to return to the days when I had been Jacques Moran. The only difference between "now" and the time before was that now I didn't have the money to finance a trip to the West. Part of me said, "Oh, never mind about money! All you need is the one-way fare, and what's wrong with third class?" However, I'd experienced severe neurasthenia, and I didn't have the courage to go without money. It may just be because I'm a Japanese, but, while I thought, on the one hand, that I was sick of the Orient and wanted to travel to the West and finally die there, I also considered that without money I wouldn't be able to enjoy drinking fine wines or eating delicious foods. I had started to make a good recovery now, but what if I got thinner and thinner, and what if those panic attacks began again? Such were my fears. So I told Shigeko to "put up with my absence for a few years. I don't know where I'm going to go, but if I survive, I'll probably come back at some point." Then, with a little less than two thousand yen in my pocket, I set off for Shanghai. My initial thought was that, if I got to Shanghai, a wonderful Western style of life awaited me. There might even be more pleasures available to me than in Paris, in a sense. So I would put up with Shanghai for a certain period of time and monitor the state of my health carefully. When I was sure everything was all right, that my panic attacks weren't coming back, and that I wasn't feeling homesick, I would wait for a chance to go again to the West. Soon after I arrived in Shanghai, however, I used up my two thousand yen.

Fortunately, though, just then an alluring American woman fell for me in a big way, and I became a pimp. I daresay you know what a pimp is, but, just in case, it's a gigolo and a procurer of women combined. I was taken on by the American woman, then found two or three young girls to "run," and started on this shameful business.

I don't think I need to go into the details of the trade, but white girls of this sort, "white slaves," as they are called, can be found in every port in the Orient. The people who "run" them are in close communication with each other and cooperate to make personnel and other matters go smoothly. The women who are being "run" sometimes move between one port town and another—Yokohama, Kobe, Tianjin, Shanghai, Singapore, and Hong Kong. They move around quite a lot. Sometimes one of the "shops" will expand and have branches in several ports. I was scared of dabbling in such a business, but if you don't have work of some sort you can't eat, you know. Besides, this was the only kind of work I could actually do. And, after all, things are as you take them to be. Always surrounded with wine and women, free to do as you please, and making a lot of money in the process—what could be a more plum job than that? "And I'm all the luckier: I'll put up with this for two or three years, and then, when I've saved enough money, wash my hands of the whole business and go to the West!" That was my plan.

Time passed, and it was in the spring of 1913 that I visited Japan. The brothel at Number 10 in Yokohama, which you're acquainted with, was for sale, and the plan was for me to buy it and turn it into a branch of our place in Shanghai. So it wasn't exactly a sentimental journey home for me that time. I had come to the "market" of Yokohama, that oriental port, to do business on behalf of a white slaver. As for my name, I've forgotten to state clearly to you that I had cast aside "Matsunaga Gisuke" by the time I went to Shanghai and was using the name "Tomoda Ginzō," which I happened to pick when I first introduced myself to you. During the year I spent in Shanghai, I had a presentiment that the amazing changes in my body would begin again and I would become as fat as I once was in Paris. And my presentiment was splendidly on target! After a year of wild, unrestrained eating and drinking in Shanghai, my body ballooned like a rubber ball. I had been a scrawny 100 pounds when I left my hometown, but when I came to Yokohama I weighed over 170 pounds, the same as the record I'd set earlier. I

made a bold entry into Tokyo, and when I came to the Café Liberté
on the Ginza one evening, there you were again . . .

You're a novelist with strong imaginative powers. Having heard
this much about my strange life, I'm sure you can imagine most of
the rest. In a word, my physique has continued to transform itself
every few years. At my thinnest, 90 pounds, and my fattest, 170:
I moved back and forth between these two extremes roughly every
fourth year. When my weight fell to ninety pounds, I longed for my
dimly lit family home and felt nostalgia for everything of purely
Japanese taste. I grew sentimental, and in face, physique, and
personality I turned back into "Matsunaga Gisuke" and returned
to Yagyumura. Then, as I passed my days peacefully there, I would
slowly recover my health. First, I would develop a good healthy
appetite for my food. Then sexual desire would revive. I would grow
to dislike oriental tastes and find my passive way of life distasteful.
My weight would gradually increase to over 100 pounds. Then
I would have a premonition of sudden, radical weight gain and
hurriedly leave home. Off I'd go to Shanghai, where I'd look up some
connections I had and resume the white slave trade. In the course
of one year, my weight would go from 100 to close to 170 pounds.
I would turn into "Tomoda Ginzō," establish a branch brothel in
Yokohama, and carry on business between China and Japan . . .
From 1912 to today, in 1925, I've continued to transform in the way
I've described. What? Didn't I ever go to the West again? Are you
asking if I didn't make enough money to do so? No, I made quite a lot
of money, in fact; but in 1914 the world war broke out, and it became
difficult to get a visa. Besides, given the business I was involved in,
there was no shortage of white women to enjoy as I liked. Whether
it was Yokohama or Shanghai, wherever I happened to be was
like Paris. You can tell just how prodigal and wild I was from the
collection of photographs I used to show you. I didn't need to turn
into Jacques Moran: I got all I needed as "Tom-san"/"Tomoda
Ginzō." It was better for me that way. So, though I had meant to
wash my hands of it all at a certain point, in the end I decided to

forget about going to the West and keep on with this business. I put the money I'd made when I closed down Number 10 in 1915 into my bank account in Shanghai and used it to open Number 27 in 1919. It must have been around then that "Tomoda Ginzō" made his third appearance in Café Présantant on the Ginza . . .

(I had listened quietly to the truly amazing story of Tomoda Ginzō up to this point, but now at last I decided to ask a few questions.)

"So then, you were running both Café Présantant and Café Liberté before that?"

"No, it just happened that the Café Liberté was in operation at the same time as Number 10 and Café Présantant at the same time as Number 27. Neither of them had any connection to me. So the waiters there may have had some inklings of what kind of a person I was, but they could not have known for sure."

"Well then, why did you patronize that sort of place? As Tomoda Ginzō, you would have had no need for the society of Japanese, would you?"

"Oh yes, I see I've left out something important to the story! Whenever I heard of a particular café that you frequented, I went out of a desire to meet you. I wanted to have you, as a novelist, listen to this strange story of mine at some point. Why do you think I hid Tomoda's seal and ring and the photographs and postal card from you in that satchel that Shigeko discovered? When I turned back into Matsunaga Gisuke and went home to Yagyumura, I'd sell off everything else I had, but I never parted with the contents of that satchel. It wasn't only to keep them as souvenirs of my adventures. You never know when you might die, so, in case I was taken seriously ill in the countryside, I'd prepared things so that everything could be made clear: 'This Matsunaga person is your friend Tomoda Ginzō. He looks completely different, but here is the evidence for what I say.'

"But, you may ask, 'Why didn't you confess the truth that time

when I pressed you for it at the Café Présentant?' Well, the way you handled it then seemed to me too much like an ambush. You shoved in my face that photograph of me in pilgrim dress. Your manner suggested that you already knew at least half of my secret. I was at first surprised and then felt hostile toward you. And not only that—I was angry with Shigeko for having the nerve to write you a letter about me. I had no idea that she had examined the contents of that satchel on the sly until I heard what you had to say. I think it was only natural that I showed some stubbornness about the matter."

"And that time later, when we met at Number 27—you were still being stubborn?"

"That night I was really terrified. It started with being asked about my hometown: I was tortured by the premonition that my panic attacks would begin again and I'd immediately start losing weight. I tried to hide my fear by drinking a lot that evening, but the panic attacks did start again the next day. I began to lose weight and in a year had turned back into Matsunaga Gisuke."

"So you're saying that the Matsunaga Gisuke whom I met in Yagyumura three years ago was actually you, now here in front me?"

"Yes, precisely.— But no, perhaps not . . ." Having said which, Tomoda Ginzō set down his glass of cognac, the last of many he had drunk. "The man Matsunaga Gisuke and the man Tomoda Ginzō may be quite distinct persons after all. They have different personalities, and when one of them is in this world, the other is not. And they take possession of this 'me' in alternation. That's the only way I can see it."

He stretched out one hand and showed me his amethyst ring: "Now look at this. At present I am Tomoda Ginzō—certainly not Matsunaga Gisuke. I always estimate my weight by means of this ring. When it digs into the flesh of my finger and can't be taken off, my weight is close to 170 pounds, at least."

"So you're now moving between Shanghai and Yokohama on the same kind of business?"

"The earthquake finished off the shop in Yokohama, so I've opened one in Kobe. But I wonder what will become of me in the end? How long will I keep repeating the Tomoda Ginzō and Matsunaga Gisuke transformations? I'm forty-five this year, and I'll turn into Matsunaga Gisuke in another three or four years. After that, Tomoda Ginzō just might not come back. That's what I feel, somehow. This last time, when I left Japan behind, I felt the panic attacks might recur earlier than usual, and I made a point of spending more time in Yokohama than in Shanghai. And Kobe is even closer to Matsunaga Gisuke's hometown, after all . . ."

Tomoda Ginzō looked a little sad as he said this; but even so, he seemed to me to be three or four years younger than forty-five.

A NIGHT IN QINHUAI

Translated by Anthony H. Chambers

At five-thirty in the afternoon I returned briefly to my inn, south of the Stone Slab Bridge, but it seemed a shame to stay holed up on the second floor when the night promised a splendid moon. Impatient to see the riverfront road at Qinhuai one more time, I took a quick bath, arranged for a guide, and called for two rickshaws.

"But your dinner is ready, sir. Why don't you wait until you've eaten?" The maid looked at me in surprise, as if she wondered where on earth I might be going.

"That's all right, I'll eat outside. I'm going to have Chinese food tonight."

With no hesitation I changed into Western clothes and went downstairs.

"Chinese food tonight, sir?" The guide grinned when he saw me. He was an attractive Chinese man of thirty-seven or -eight and spoke Japanese well. A bright fellow, he had learned Japanese ways; apparently he planned to go to Japan soon and start a ceramics business. During this trip to China, I had been offended by the unhelpfulness and laziness of my guides, but this fellow was an exception. He was well educated and, as a native of the place, was familiar with local legends and folklore, making him incomparably superior to an uninformed Japanese guide. It is also true that the traveler is free to indulge in foolish pleasures when his companion is Chinese because he need not feel any silly constraints. If you can get your inn to find someone reliable—for not all Chinese people are dishonest—a Chinese guide is best.

"Where shall we go for Chinese food, sir? There are some places in this neighborhood, but . . ."

"There's nothing of interest in this neighborhood. Let's go to Qinhuai again."

Presently our two rickshaws, with my guide in the lead, headed due south along the avenue that runs in front of the inn.

The sun had set. Unlike cities in Japan, Chinese cities, whether Beijing or Nanjing, are deserted once night falls. With no trams running and no streetlights burning, the roads are utterly silent, and not a glimmer of light escapes from the houses, enclosed as they are behind thick walls of plaster or stone, with no windows visible and their narrow, wooden doors firmly shut. Even in lively areas, comparable to the Ginza in Tokyo, most businesses close at six or seven o'clock; and in the neighborhood around the inn, consisting entirely of residences, the empty streets were as hushed as in the dead of night, even at a few minutes past six. Apparently the moon had not yet risen, but, unfortunately, scattered rain clouds drifting across the sky suggested that the view would not be what I hoped for. Aside from the dull rumble of our rickshaws (Chinese models almost never have rubber wheels), nothing disturbed the solitude of the surroundings except the rare clip-clop of a one-horse carriage. The lamps on these carriages only illuminated about one foot of the ground, and the interior of the cabs was pitch dark. As we passed each other, there might be, in the darkness, a slight illumination in the glass, and then it was gone.

At the intersection where the Luzheng Gate stands, our rickshaws turned left into an even darker, more desolate street. Crumbling brick walls towered on both sides, zigzagging in and out, again and again, and the rickshaws, too, turned again and again as they ran between the walls. I feared that the walls might close in on us from both sides and that we were about to crash into one of them. If I were left stranded in a place like this, I would never get back to the inn, even if I spent all night trying. Suddenly the walls ended and we came to a vacant lot. It gaped like a missing tooth among the walls around it. In the lot stood heaps of rubble, as if this had been the site of a fire, and a pool of water, which could have been a marsh or an old pond. Vacant lots are not unusual in Chinese cities, even in the center of town, and they are especially common in Nanjing. In the Tangzi Lane area, north of Rouqiao Avenue, which I had traversed during the day, there were many pools of water with countless geese swimming in them. Perhaps this is the sort of thing that makes an old capital an old capital.

Just as I was thinking that we had ridden rather far, we emerged into another broad avenue. Even so, it was barely as wide as Nakadōri in Nihonbashi. The buildings on both sides appeared to be shops, but not a single door was open. Then I saw a monumental gate in the center of the road, with the words "Blossom Gate" inscribed on a white tablet, barely legible in the darkness.

"This area is called the Blossom Neighborhood, isn't it?" I yelled to the guide from my rickshaw.

"That's right," he shouted from the rickshaw in front. "In the old days, when this was the Ming capital, the artisans who made clothing for the ladies and officials of the court lived here. If you had come here then, you would have seen beautiful robes spread out everywhere and artisans, in every house, embroidering gorgeous blossoms on them with colorful silk thread. That's why the area is called the Blossom Neighborhood."

Suddenly this dark street felt dear to me. Could it be that, even now, inside those silent doors, artisans had spread out dazzling robes and were patiently applying their needles to exquisite embroidery? . . .

While I was lost in this reverie, the rickshaws passed Taiping Lane and Liumi Lane and then crossed Sixiang Bridge. The Qinhuai Confucian Temple would be nearby. I must have passed here during the day, but I still had no sense of direction. The road narrowed again, and the rickshaws were constantly arriving at walls and cutting across vacant lots. Traversing what must have been a road with a long wall on the right side, we turned right and left, again and again, and finally emerged from Yaojia Alley onto the road along the Qinhuai River. The Confucian Temple stands two or three blocks farther down this road. During the day the area is alive with male and female visitors weaving in and out; there are stalls offering sweets, fruit, and sundries, and such attractions as acrobats and serpent sideshows, all standing in festive rows; but recently, as the police have grown more strict, the shows and stalls have been shutting down at six o'clock in the evening. Apparently the nights are deserted because of the many soldiers who entered the city in the tumult of the revolution. People say that the most dangerous men in China are the soldiers. In my experience, too, the local people are quite gentle, and I have never seen them behaving badly. Only soldiers present a threat. A great many of them have entered Beijing and Tianjin, as well, where they crowd the streets at night. The rule is that soldiers, and only soldiers, are allowed to make merry in theaters and brothels without paying, and so naturally other customers have stopped going to these places. Entertainment districts therefore make no money in towns that are dominated by soldiers. One hears of "the tumult of revolution," but this area is extremely tranquil now, and so it is a mystery why troops need to be stationed here. In their idleness, they do nothing but occupy famous Buddhist temples in the cities, using them as barracks and making everyone anxious. Nanjing is probably more accursed by their presence than any other city.

It would seem, however, that restaurants do not admit soldiers for free, since first-rate Nanjing establishments, lining the two or three blocks from the foot of Lishe Bridge to the corner of Examination Hall West Road, stay open late into the night. Our rickshaws came to a stop before one of these, a restaurant called Zhangsong Donghao.

"Let's go in here. They serve authentic Nanjing cuisine." As he spoke, my guide entered ahead of me. The interior was much finer than the facade had led me to expect. A spacious, rectangular court-yard in the center was surrounded on four sides by a high, two-story structure. Though it was a wooden house, painted green, the work-manship was far from shoddy. Delicate carvings adorned the railings and posts along the second-floor corridors, and the columns were decorated with paper lanterns and potted chrysanthemums in full bloom. As I stood in the courtyard and surveyed the upper and lower floors, every room was occupied with guests, who were noisily gambling and playing the finger-guessing game. I had hoped to lay claim to a second-floor room, overlooking the Qinhuai Canal, but we were told that the only available room was downstairs, just to the right of the entrance. I decided to make do with that, and the room was very comfortable once we were settled inside. In Beijing the interiors of even first-class places are filthy, but tonight I felt that I would finally be able enjoy some delicious food without any worries. Having consumed a fair amount of Chinese food in Japan, I chose the following dishes by myself from the menu that the waiter brought.

醋溜黃魚　yellow croaker drizzled with vinegar
炒山鷄　stir-fried pheasant
炒蝦仁　stir-fried shrimp
鍋鴨舌　duck-tongue hot pot

We also had a variety of cold dishes and mushroom soup. My impression is that the cuisines of South China and Beijing use generally the same ingredients, but their flavors are markedly different. This impression was especially strong when I tasted the first dish to appear, the stir-fried shrimp. The raw material must be of good quality, since they say shrimp is a specialty of this region, but more important, the seasoning was wonderfully simple. I doubt that even Japanese cuisine could match its lightness. Even a person who hates Chinese food would surely not reject this dish.

"How about it? I've heard there are a lot of geisha houses on the opposite bank. Are there many beauties in them?" I offered more

Shaoxing wine and looked out over the water as I spoke. My Chinese guide, a little tipsy now, answered with an engaging smile on his red face.

"Yes, there are some. Most Japanese gentlemen summon a geisha once for the experience. Why don't you call one here? Three dollars will be enough to have her sing for you."

"I'm not interested in having her come and sing. Wouldn't it be better for us to go to a geisha house after we've finished here? If there's one you know, please take me."

"Yes, that would be fun." He nodded with a smile in his eyes and a knowing look. "That would be fun, but there are no women in the houses on the opposite bank, because the soldiers get out of hand. The houses you can see from here are all vacant, and the women have fled to dark, isolated alleys where the troops don't go. They're rather hard to find."

This reply only excited my curiosity further. "But you must know at least one such place. An isolated spot like that would be all the more interesting, wouldn't it?"

He laughed. "Oh, I'm sure we'll find one if we look. All right, I'll take you."

We ate heartily as we chatted. I had been famished when I left the inn, but now I was stuffed, despite having been born a heavy eater. The rooms next to us and across the courtyard were still noisy. The night was gradually darkening, but angry shouts from those playing at finger guessing and the jangle of silver coins being pushed about by gamblers engrossed in their games echoed around us as if to overwhelm the waters of the Qinhuai.

"This is nothing compared to the summertime. The restaurants and geisha houses are packed with guests, night after night, and the canal is filled with pleasure boats bearing people who sing and play the *erhu*. It's very lively. Now that the weather has grown cold, there are fewer guests than usual."

"When are the pleasure boats busiest?"

"Let's see. Roughly from the beginning of spring, in March or April, to the end of September."

I regretted not having come a month earlier. On a quiet night like this, I was unable to savor fully the atmosphere of South China that I had been looking forward to. I would have to come again, when the weather was warm.

"That was a wonderful dinner. Thanks to you, I'm feeling quite mellow. Perhaps we should go soon." My guide had finished off the second bottle of Shaoxing wine and was studying my expression as he spoke. A great deal of food remained on the table, but neither of us had the courage to touch it. When we summoned the waiter and looked at our check, the total was only two dollars. This was extremely cheap, considering that we had stuffed ourselves. Such a meal would cost seven or eight yen at a Chinese restaurant in Japan. Western and Japanese dishes are unpalatable and expensive in China. The Japanese food prepared by Chinese chefs, in particular, is unspeakably bad. Dining on Chinese cuisine is more enjoyable and economical, even if the stuff is not quite clean.

It must have been after ten o'clock when we returned to our rickshaws in front of the restaurant. Following the riverside road eastward, we came to Lishe Bridge, under which I had passed by pleasure boat during the day. In Nanjing, houses crowd both ends of most of the bridges, so that, unless you can see the water, you cannot be sure where the bridge begins; but the bridges spanning the Qinhuai are exceptions to this rule. The Wende, Wuding, and Lishe bridges are built of wood, like bridges in rural Japan; when I had seen them in the daylight, their steel railings were covered with Chinese cabbages set out to dry. Restaurants lined the riverbank on this side, and on the opposite bank lay a pleasure quarter with many brothels standing in jagged rows, very much as at Dōtonbori, in Osaka; but as my guide had predicted, every house was pitch dark and firmly locked up. At some point the moon had come out, its pale light breaking through the lightly overcast sky to cast a weak glow on the leaden, sleepy waters of the canal; but aside from that, the gloomy streets stretched on and on as if they were dead. Arriving at the north end of Lishe Bridge, our rickshaws seemed to be sucked into the darkness of the quarter as they turned down the road to the left. Strangely, even when we drew close to the row of riverside brothels that we had seen from the opposite bank, it still was not clear where their entrances were. As before, we went in and out of narrow alleys surrounded by earthen walls. Gradually the way narrowed until only one rickshaw at a time could get through, and the surface was paved unevenly with stones about the size of bricks. Jolted violently as we banged and crashed along, we went around so many walled corners that I no longer knew in which direction the river lay. Presently we came to a bend in the road so narrow that a rickshaw could not get through, and so, telling the men to wait, my guide and I walked together along the wall. It was an awful road, with jagged, protruding cobblestones that threatened to catch the heel of my shoe and send me sprawling. Dark liquid trickled here and there; I could not be sure whether it was urine or cooking oil. On the white wall—or I should say on the surface of the dirty gray, stained, earthen wall—the moon cast a misty light, illuminating the wall faintly, as in a night scene from a motion picture. Come to think of it, the alley looked just like those back streets one often sees in Western motion pictures, into which villainous underlings flee and detectives follow. There is no telling what might have become of me if I had become lost in such a place and my Chinese guide had been some kind of criminal. It was frightening to contemplate.

"Are you sure there are geisha houses in a place like this?" I whispered into the guide's ear.

"Yes, just wait a bit. I think there's one around here," he replied softly. For some reason he was pacing back and forth in the same spot. Or maybe it was not just one spot, but the street was so obscure that it might as well have been so. Finally we came to a house on the right side, its six-foot-wide entrance open and a lamp burning brightly. Apparently the occupants sold food, for warm smoke rose thickly from an oven, just as at a baked sweet potato vendor's. Passing before it, we went another five or six yards, where the road turned again, sharply to the left. Leaving me there, my guide backtracked to the smoky shop, where he seemed to be questioning someone at great length. His face, illuminated by the lamp at the shop entrance, floated red in the darkness. Then he came straight back to me, humming cheerfully, and walked on ahead.

"Here it is," he said, coming to a stop. "Let's go inside." We had gone only five or six paces. On the wall at the right-hand side flickered a tiny, square lamp, which looked as though it might go out at any moment. "Suzhou Hall of Fragrant Exaltation" was written in red on the glass, in letters that were peeling but legible. Below the lamp was a doorway, barely wide enough for a person to squeeze through. This "doorway" consisted of an opening that had been cut in the two- or three-foot-thick wall with a wooden door hung beyond it, and so neither voices nor lamplight escaped from inside; if you did not look carefully you would think it was simply a recess in the earthen wall. This explained why the walls had seemed to stretch on and on, with no entrances in sight. When I was about to reach out and open the door, I was surprised to find a person moving slightly in front of it. Enveloped by the deep shadow cast in the recess by the thickness of the wall, he stood still, like a statue in a niche, leaning against the door. No doubt he was a lookout of some kind. When my guide spoke a few words to him, the man gave a quick nod and opened the wooden door with a scraping sound.

The interior, too, was very dim. —Nanjing has electricity, but I am told that these houses purposely use oil lamps instead, for fear of attracting the attention of unruly soldiers. —Passing through a room in which four or five evil-looking men sat around a table, no doubt gambling, I came to the courtyard that is a feature of all houses of this type, and on the far side I saw the curtained entrances of two or three women's rooms. The room I was led to was on the far left.

There was hardly anything resembling decoration in the room. Cheap, shiny wallpaper that looked like wrapping paper hung on the walls. Even this wallpaper showed its age; though shiny, it was as coarse as a wall that wants a final coat of plaster. I remember a rosewood table and two or three chairs standing off to one side; and the only illumination was provided by a smoldering table lamp whose light could not penetrate to the corners of the room, resulting in a gloominess you would not expect in the bedroom of a woman of this sort. There was no one in the room at first, and so I sat and waited. Presently an old woman dressed in indigo, who appeared to be the madam, came in bearing a tray of watermelon and pumpkin seeds. She did not have a particularly avaricious look but smiled at me pleasantly as she chattered away incomprehensibly in Chinese. Then the lady of the bedroom entered gracefully, followed by two girls of twelve or thirteen. No sooner had she occupied the chair between my guide and me than she propped one elbow on the table and extended her other arm to offer us cigarettes. When I questioned her, with my guide interpreting, she replied that she was eighteen this year and her name was Qiao. Her plump, round face was so white in the feeble lamplight that it shone. The delicate flesh of her nostrils was a pale, translucent red. Even more beautiful were her glossy hair, blacker yet than the black satin garment she wore, and the expression in her lively eyes, infinitely charming and open wide, as if she were surprised. I had met many women in Beijing, but I had never seen one as beautiful as this. It was incomprehensible that such a smoothly polished woman should live within such dim, filthy walls. *Polished* is probably the most appropriate word to describe this woman's charms. Though her features departed little from those of the typical beauty, the luster of her skin, the movement of her eyes, the way she did her hair, her general bearing—all of these perfectly displayed the highly refined appeal of one brought up to be a geisha. Her eyes and hands were never still while she spoke. She constantly changed her posture. Moving her head, bouncing the rich forelocks that covered her forehead and her gold earrings, shaped like blossoms with bits of jade at the tips, she would suddenly pull in her plump chin and look as if she were lost in thought; extend her elbows to the side and draw up her shoulders; and, finally, pulling out the golden hairpin with which she fastened her hair at the back and using it as a toothpick, display her wonderful row of teeth, which was especially polished among the "polished."

My guide had been ignoring me as he joked with the woman and smoked a hookah with a pipe borrowed from the old lady; but suddenly he turned to me and said, "What do you think? She's a beauty, isn't she? The classiest geisha in the area. I've been negotiating with her. If you like her, what would you think of spending the night?"

"Has she agreed to that?"

"No, she won't consent that easily. But I'm negotiating now, and you'll probably be able to stay."

"Yes, by all means, please make it possible."

She taunted me with a sidelong glance.

My guide reopened the talks. It all seemed a little too playful to be a negotiation, but I had no choice but to wait silently for the outcome. Leaning back against the wall, I gazed attentively at the woman's animated expressions as they changed from one to the next.

She would appear to be playful, and then, with a serious look, she would lift those round eyes and stare at the ceiling. For all his joking, the guide seemed to be doing everything he could to persuade her.

"The negotiations look difficult. How's it going?"

"She says she can't stay with you because she has another customer. But give me a few more minutes. She may come around soon."

Mollifying me with these words, he continued the negotiations. Presently the woman left the room, saying, "I'll ask," and giving me a contemptuous smile. Two or three minutes later the old madam came in, grinning. She and the guide haggled for a long time. It looked as though she could not easily refuse in the face of my guide's tenacity. Finally she withdrew, at her wits' end. Then the woman came back and made all kinds of excuses. She and the old lady took turns, going in and out several times; it seemed the matter would not be settled easily.

It looked hopeless. "If it's that much trouble, let's give up," I said, restraining the guide. The night was growing late and cold, and I was beginning to lose interest. And then, even if the negotiations were successful, I would feel uneasy, left all alone in a room in this gloomy, dubious brothel—unless, of course, the guide was willing to stay, too.

"All right, let's give up and go to another house. I've been offering fifteen dollars, but they insist on forty. For forty dollars, I think they'd agree. It's idiotic. Forty dollars is far too much. It would be better to quit."

The market for silver being high at the time, forty dollars would come to about eighty Japanese yen. I was carrying a little more than sixty dollars, but if I used forty of them here, I would have only twenty dollars with which to see the sights in Suzhou before calling at the Zhengjin Bank in Shanghai. Having already begun to lose interest, I did not feel like making such a sacrifice for this woman.

"She's a beauty, to be sure, but forty dollars is too high. It's already past eleven o'clock. Let's call it a night and go back. It was enough just to see her." I rose from my seat and spoke decisively.

"There's no need to go back yet. If this woman won't do, there are other places with beautiful women, places where you can enjoy yourself without spending forty dollars." Perhaps the guide thought I was uncommonly dissolute; his eagerness was a little annoying.

"But there can't be many as beautiful as this." I was loath to be dragged off to some strange place that would tarnish my image of this beautiful woman. I would have preferred to turn back, cherishing in my breast the figure of this woman, so like a noble dream.

"Well, let's go and see whether there are any other beauties. You can always return to the inn and sleep if they don't please you. It doesn't matter if you stay out late." The woman had seen us to the door and locked it from the inside when my guide spoke and started to trudge on along the paving stones of the alley. Ten or twelve yards beyond stood another house that appeared to be a brothel. Like the first one, it was surrounded by a heavy, thick wall, and its little side door was locked as darkly and silently as a prison gate. The guide went in by himself, but he quickly emerged, saying, "No beauties here. There must be other places." Indeed, if one looked closely, houses that appeared to be women's hideaways stood here and there. They say the women fled here because they were afraid of violent soldiers, but the houses were exceedingly wretched compared with the prosperity of the Eight Great Hutongs in Beijing. They had something of the feel of the streets behind the Suiten Shrine in Tokyo. My guide would stop before each of them, give a doubtful look, and hurry on.

"There don't seem to be any good houses around here. Let's go someplace else, by rickshaw." Mumbling under his breath, he backtracked to the road we had taken before. There was no sign of our rickshaws. We had taken a circuitous route between earthen walls, turning again and again, and aside from us no human form was to be seen loitering in the area. It was like wandering among dismal ruins. The only human forms roaming in such a place on a dark night like this would surely have been ghosts. In fact the alley looked more suitable as a dwelling place for specters than for humans.

It was when we turned from a narrow alley into a slightly wider one that we finally found a rickshaw. A food stand had been set up there, rather like those that offer noodle stew in Japan, and a rickshaw man was poking at fried rice or something. (This stand was a mystery to me. For whom was their food intended? Only a ghost would come here to eat. In fact, the old man running it may have been a ghost.) The guide had me climb into the rickshaw and followed us on foot. Now and then he would give directions, yelling, "Turn right!" or "Go left!" from behind me. Probably he, too, had no clear idea yet of where we would go next.

Two or three blocks later the guide found another rickshaw. Our two vehicles finally emerged from the ruins and clattered into a city street. Somehow it looked familiar, but I still had no sense of where we might be. On the left side stood a shop with a sign reading "Taibai's Legacy." I looked carefully as we passed. A number of large casks lay in a row, blackened with soot like those in a countryside soy sauce warehouse. The place resembled an oil shop as well, but judging from the name Taibai's Legacy it was probably a wine vendor's. I thought of Satō Haruo's story "Li Taibai." No doubt Satō would be interested to hear about this shop sign.[1]

Ten or twelve yards ahead stood a gate resembling the Main Gate of the Yoshiwara district, with the words "Qinhuai Bridge" dimly legible atop it.[2] Recognizing the name, I knew I must have passed this way in the morning, too. I had left the restaurant near the Confucius Temple just a short time before, and now, before I knew it, I had been transported here again. The rickshaws crossed the Qinhuai Bridge and seemed to be heading back toward the Confucius Temple. When they came again to the foot of Lishe Bridge, however, the rickshaw men did not turn toward the temple but went straight across the bridge and broke into a run. I had come as far as this bridge before, but tonight I was crossing it to the opposite bank for the first time. As I wondered what sorts of neighborhoods lay ahead, we turned right on the riverfront road, and then turned left. The moon had gone down and the darkness was even thicker than before, and so it was impossible to see what kind of neighborhood we were traversing. I could only make out the usual grim, cold, gray walls running on silently, like the stone ramparts of an old castle, interspersed here and there with weed-filled vacant lots. It was clear that we were heading into the outskirts, toward more and more desolate places. When the walls ended and we came to open land, a damp, cold, night breeze flowed stealthily toward me from nowhere in particular. The

---

1. "Taibai" refers to the Tang poet Li Taibai, or Li Bai (also called Li Bo, 701–62), a famous drinker. Tanizaki's friend Satō Haruo (佐藤春夫, 1892–1964) published his short story "Li Taibai" (李太白 or "Ri Taihaku" in Japanese) in 1918.

2. Yoshiwara was the main prostitution quarter in Tokyo.

more these gloomy surroundings sank into me, the more vividly the image of the beautiful woman I had seen just thirty minutes before rose in my breast. No matter how much I thought it over, I could only believe that encountering such a beauty in that forsaken city had been like a dream. It seemed a shame now that I had begrudged those forty dollars.

With a thud, my rickshaw bounced violently and turned right into a dreadfully uneven road. On the left were clustered two or three houses, and on the right was an old pond. Five or six ancient willows grew at the edge of the pond, trailing their leafy branches like a black curtain, whispering in the breeze. The water in the pond shone leadenly and seemed to quiver with the willow leaves. Our rickshaws came to a stop before the last house on the left. I could pick out "—House" on the lamp burning at the door, but the red of the first two characters had peeled off.

The entrance was even darker and more obscure than that of the previous house. When my guide rapped softly at the door, part of the wall receded, as if into a cavern, and sucked us inside; but the gloom of outdoors extended inside as well, and so one could not be sure where the interior began. Hearing the door scrape closed behind us, I turned to look back, but there was only darkness before my eyes. I could neither make out the door through which we must have just come nor even see the person who must have opened it for us. Outdoors there had at least been willows and a pond, but inside there was nothing but darkness. We had definitely come from the far side of the wall to this side, but when and how had we passed through it to a place like this? Peering at the darkness behind me, I felt as though there were no wall there at all. The world of the pond and willows was sternly concealed by a "wall of darkness" even thicker than the earthen wall. I recalled that, as a child, I had often experienced the same sensation when I exited into a dark corridor after viewing the Panorama.[3]

---

3. Japan's first panorama was erected in Ueno Park, Tokyo, in 1890, when Tanizaki was four years old. See http://www.meijitaisho.net/toa/panoramakan.php.

Then, from the bottom of the darkness that covered everything before me, came another scraping sound. The entrance was doubly enclosed, with a second, wooden door ahead of me. A black human shadow seemed to be wobbling toward me like a bat; weak lamplight fell on its back from beyond the wooden door. My imagination leaped to a horrible scene. What if I were threatened by a hoodlum in this pitch-dark house, which I had entered but whose final exit I did not know? It might not end with threats—if I were killed and my corpse disposed of, the crime would go forever undiscovered. Inside the four walls of this brothel, this fiendish lair, I was as cut off from normal society as I would have been at the bottom of the sea.

After exchanging whispers with the man, my guide led me to the far side of the wooden door. The arrangement of bedrooms enclosing a central courtyard on four sides was similar to the design of the previous house, but both the area of the courtyard and the number of bedrooms seemed much larger here. In the center of the stone-paved yard sat a crude, low table, where five or six girls, their shoulders hunched against the cold, were slurping rice porridge and nibbling pickled vegetables that looked like *fukujinzuke*. Their furtive, pathetic manner was just like that of rats eating under the veranda of a storehouse. Peering into two or three bedrooms, the guide selected the one that looked cleanest and appropriated it for our use. Here, too, an oil lamp was burning, and, perhaps because we had passed through an exceedingly dark space, the room was surprisingly bright. This does not mean that the dreary atmosphere inside was enlivened by the brightness. Other than a woman's bed on one side, screened by white curtains, and the usual table and chairs on the other side, there was nothing at all by way of decoration. Peeking at the bed through slits in the curtains, I saw a blanket rolled loosely on top of a grimy pad. Wondering if anyone were lying there, I moved the blanket a bit, and the tip of a charming satin slipper peeped out from the edge like an acorn. What a petite, delicate woman lies here, I sensed, just from glimpsing the tip of the slipper. One would expect the supple, rattan mesh stretched across the bottom of the bed to sag a little when someone was sleeping on it, but under the woman's light body this bed was taut, as oblivious to her weight as if a ball of cotton lay there.

"Here, here, why don't you get up?" Speaking in Japanese, I put my hands on the blanket and shook. My fingers felt her lithe flesh distinctly under the blanket—her arms, her breast, her legs—as if they were touching her naked body. Rubbing her eyes, she threw off the blanket and sat up wearily.—Wearing a pale-green cotton jacket, she had a dark complexion, the protruding eyes of a goldfish, thick, curling lips, and a dimwitted expression. With her hands inside her jacket, she shivered as she crawled out of bed and sat next to me, where she began to chew pumpkin seeds with a sullen look.

"How about this woman? You don't like her? If you don't like her, there are many others in this house. Let's call another one."

I could not conceal my dissatisfaction with this woman's appearance, so inferior it was to the beautiful woman I had met earlier.

"In that case, we should ask to have a look at them. After we've seen them all, we can request the best one, right?"

"Right. You can look as much as you like."

The women who had been slurping porridge in the courtyard soon presented themselves to me, one by one. Lifting a curtain that hung in front of her bedroom, like the *agemaku* on a stage, each would walk toward me like a marionette, strike a flirtatious pose, and then withdraw quietly behind the curtain. The display had something of the quality of an *oiran* courtesan's introduction to a new client. More than ten women filed toward me, but none appealed to me in the slightest. Every one of them looked unclean, just like a rat. On balance, the first had been the best.

"However you look at it, sir, she's the most beautiful. Will she do?"

"But her clothes and her face are much worse than the woman in the other house."

"There's nothing we can do about that. You won't find many women as beautiful as that first one. She's conceited because she's a first-rate geisha. This place is second rate, but that means there's no problem about spending the night. And I'm sure they'll give you a good price since they're suffering from the bad economy."

Understanding the gist of what the guide had said, the woman set about seducing me; but the harder she tried, the less interested I became. She said her name was Chen Xiuxiang, and her age was nineteen. Though her face could have been worse, her clothing was filthy and, worst of all, the coarseness of her skin was distasteful to me. As I stared at this woman's rough, lusterless fingers, the beautiful complexion of that other woman, polished like lapis lazuli, came to seem more and more unforgettable.

"How about it, sir? Why don't you spend the night? They say they'll come down to twelve dollars."

"No, let's give up. I just don't like her. Tonight I'd rather go back to the inn and sleep."

"Really? Back to the inn?" The guide saw the displeasure in my face and seemed embarrassed. "Let's try one more place on the way back. If it's no good, then we'll go on to the inn."

"All right, if it's on the way back; but it'll just be more of the same, won't it? We're not going to find another beauty like the first one, wherever we go."

He laughed. "You've really fallen for her, haven't you, sir? Well, I'll find someone for you who's just as appealing. Geishas cost too much, but there are beautiful, inexpensive amateurs, too."

"Are there amateurs who will take guests, then?"

"Yes, there are women who will secretly take guests. Even Chinese men can't go to these places without an introduction. I know a house. Let's go there and see what they say."

Breaking away from her as she begged me to stay the night, we left her room, crossed the courtyard again, and plunged into the inky darkness. When I had finally passed from inside the wall where the double doors hung to the road at the edge of the pond, I heaved a sigh of relief.

The third house we visited, that of the "amateur woman," was in a confusing district of cramped, entangled lanes, apparently on the way from the Confucius Temple to Sixiang Bridge. I remember returning north from Lishe Bridge and following the narrow Yaojia Alley along the wall of the police station, but it is unclear to me where we went after that. When I think about the route that later took us back to the inn, however, I think the house was probably at the end of a cul-de-sac south of Sixiang Bridge. According to a map of Nanjing, the site is called Xiwang Street and is located directly behind the police station. It is daring of them to conduct a secret enterprise so near the police, but perhaps the Chinese officers are not very strict about these matters. From the outside, too, both the police station and the woman's house were surrounded by dreary earthen walls and stood in what seemed to be a residential neighborhood. Since even the house of a first-rate geisha was so gloomy, the darkness and desolation of the amateur's house goes without saying. Not only the darkness but also the piercing cold of the night air lapped on the stone floor inside; and in a corner of the flameless, empty, cavelike room, a girl of sixteen or seventeen stood like a wooden buddha enshrined in a forsaken temple, her chin shivering in the cold as her shining eyes reacted anxiously to the intrusion of a strange gentleman from a foreign land. Her eyes were wide slits, not round and protruding in the Chinese manner, nor were they lively, but they were moist with an unfathomable sorrow. Standing there silently, knitting her thick eyebrows with a stubborn, irritable look, she was not much inferior in appearance to the beautiful woman at the first house. Her skin was a dark, reddish brown, but its texture was infinitely smooth, and her limbs, wrapped in a black satin robe, were as graceful as a koi. Her thin, delicate, dark features, such as one sees on Japanese beauties, could not match the coquetry of that other woman; but if the other was a ruby, this woman had the melancholy of obsidian. In her laconic way, she replied reluctantly that she was seventeen, was called Hua Yuelou, and was a native of Yangzhou.

"Yes, she is a beauty. But she's in a foul mood. Doesn't she look angry to you?"

"She's not angry at all. She's just self-conscious because she's an amateur. I'm sure she'll agree if you want to stay the night."

At that point her scowl grew even more severe and, clutching my guide, she began to mutter complaints about something. Her damp eyes seemed about to release a stream of tears.

"It doesn't look like she's going to agree. She's asking us to leave, isn't she?"

But my guess was completely wrong. According to my guide, the girl was pleading with us to spend the night. "She says she's in a bad way because she has no guests, thanks to the troubled times. At first she asked for ten dollars, but now she says she'll come down to six. If I haggle, I'm sure she'll lower it to three. Three dollars would be a bargain, don't you think?"

Presently the madam came in and added her voice to the girl's pleas. They finally agreed on three dollars, as the guide had said.

When the talks were settled and my guide and the old lady had withdrawn to another room, the woman bolted the wooden door at the entrance and secured it with a bar. Then, chattering away in Chinese, she favored me with a bright smile for the first time. Her eyes and mouth, which had been shadowed by melancholy, were surprisingly expressive as she did her best to flirt with me. Unable to understand a word of Chinese, I felt sad that I lacked the means to reciprocate her sweet flirtations.

"Hua Yuelou, Hua Yuelou," I repeated, faintly pronouncing her name in the Chinese way, as I held her slender face in my hands. Her face was so small and adorable it disappeared completely between my palms. It seemed as if its pliant structure would collapse if I pressed with all my strength. Her features showed the balance of an adult's and the freshness of an infant's. Suddenly I was overcome with a powerful emotion—I never wanted to let go of the face I was holding.

◼

THE MAGICIAN

Translated by Anthony H. Chambers

◼

I no longer remember in what city it was, or in which country, that I met the magician. Sometimes I think it was in Tokyo, Japan, but at other times I feel it must have been in a colonial land in the South Seas or South America, or at a port in India or China. In any case, it was in a country far removed from Europe—the center of civilization—at a remote corner of the globe, in an extremely busy night district of an extraordinarily prosperous town. To help you form a more focused idea of the nature, spectacle, and atmosphere of the place, I will just say that it was a public area resembling the Sixth District in Asakusa but even more mysterious, chaotic, and turbulent.

If my representation that the district resembles Asakusa Park stirs in you feelings neither of beauty nor of longing but makes you think rather of a disagreeable, feculent place, this is because your concept of "beauty" differs completely from mine. Of course when I speak of beauty I do not refer to that group of "venal nymphs" who dwell beneath the Twelve-Story Tower.[1] What I am addressing is the spirit of the park as a whole. Concealing dark caverns in the

1. The Twelve-Story Tower (Ryōunkaku, "Cloud Scraping Pavilion"), which opened in 1890, symbolized the plebian pleasures of Asakusa Park in Tokyo. "Venal nymphs" is in English in the original.

background while wearing a bright, joyful expression on the surface; flashing curious, daring eyes; vaunting poisonous make-up, night after night—it is this flavor of the entire park to which I speak. I speak of the magnificent, oceanic spectacle of that gigantic park which fuses all things together—good and evil, beauty and ugliness, laughter and tears; emits an ever more dazzling light; and brims with brilliant patterns of color. And I recall that the park of which I will speak now, off in a certain land, was, in its grandeur and turbidity, a strange, brutal place, even more in the style of the Sixth District than the Sixth District itself.

If I showed that park in a certain country to those who consider Asakusa Park a disgusting, vulgar site, what would they say? Barbarity, filth, and dissolution gathered there like stagnant sewer water and, under the blazing tropical sun of day and in the lantern glow of night, were shamelessly laid bare, endlessly fermenting and exuding a humid stench. But one who understands the savor of those thousand-year-old-eggs in Chinese cuisine will cut through the peculiar, nauseating smell of the dark-green, decomposing duck egg and smack his lips over the delectable, rich flavors inside. This is exactly the sort of uncanny allure that captivated me when I first entered that park.

I think it was an evening in early summer; a cool breeze was blowing. After a pleasant rendezvous in a certain café in the city, my lover and I were strolling happily, arm in arm, along an avenue full of trams, automobiles, and rickshaws.

"Sweetheart, let's take a look at the park tonight," she whispered in my ear, opening wide her captivating eyes.

"Park? What's in the park?" I was somewhat taken aback. Not only had I been unaware of the existence of a park in that city, but I also sensed that something dubious lurked in her words, as if she were inciting me to a secret evil.

"But you'll love it. I was terrified the first time I went. I thought it was shameful for a girl my age to set foot in such a place. But after I fell in love with you, I began, under your influence, to sense an indescribable allure in such places. Even when I couldn't meet you, I began to feel as though I were with you when I went there. The park is beautiful, just as you are beautiful. It's whimsical, just as you are whimsical. Surely you know it."

"Yes, I do, I do," I replied, before I knew what I was saying. Then I added, "They have all sorts of extraordinary shows and exhibits, don't they? All the wonders of the world have been assembled: an amphitheater, such as you see in ancient Rome; Spanish bullfights; and, even more fantastic and resplendent than these, a Hippodrome. And motion pictures, which I love even more than I love you, who are so sweet and adorable! Many films are screened there like daytime phantoms, even more hair-raising than *Fantômas* and *Protéa*,[2] which have stirred the curiosity of people around the world."

"At that theater I've recently seen many motion pictures based on famous epics and plays by the antique poets and artists you're always reading. You probably know the films about Homer's *Iliad* and Dante's *Inferno*.[3] But I wonder if you've seen the seductive smile of that voluptuous demon in the Women's Kingdom of Western Liang in the Chinese novel *Journey to the West*.[4] Or if you've imagined the horror of seeing those strange tales woven from exquisite threads of terror, fancy, and mystery by the American writer Poe as they unroll on film before your eyes. You must experience the moment when that shocking cellar scene in 'The Black Cat,' or the black dungeon of 'The Pit and the Pendulum' are forcefully and brightly illuminated, even more shockingly than in the stories and more vividly than in reality. And the hundreds of people who silently watched these dramas of projected light were drenched in cold perspiration, as if they were seeing nightmares; women clung to men's arms and men grasped the women's shoulders as, clenching their teeth and shuddering, they

---

2. French films *Fantômas* and *Protéa* were released in 1913.

3. *L'Inferno* (1911) was the first full-length Italian film and the first film to show male frontal nudity.

4. *Journey to the West,* by Wu Cheng-en, was published in the 1590s.

riveted their frenzied, frightened eyes on the screen. Occasionally one of them would sigh, like a patient racked with a high fever; but no one coughed or blinked—their souls were too dumbstruck, their bodies too rigid to allow for that. Then someone finding the stimulation too much to bear would try to escape by averting his face, whereupon wild, clamorous applause would rise from somewhere in the dark seats. The applause would spread instantly, even those who had been wavering would join in, and a roar would echo through the hall as if the theater were swaying in a tremor."

Word by word, her masterly, provocative narrative aroused in my breast a lucid, detailed phantasm, like a rainbow in the firmament, and I sensed a kind of radiance, as if I were watching a film rather than listening to a story. I also felt as though I had visited the park any number of times. At the very least, the many films she said she had seen appeared again and again, indistinctly, neither delusions nor photographs, on the walls of my mind and encouraged my scrutiny.

"But in that park there must be something that shall torment our souls even more keenly and captivate our senses anew—an unprecedented performance that even a curiosity seeker like me has never dreamt of. I don't know what that might be, but surely you know."

"Yes," she replied immediately. "I know. It would be the beautiful young magician who recently opened a theater at the edge of a lake in the park.

"The local people say the magician's figure and face are so radiant that it's safest for anyone who has a lover to stay away. Many say the magic in his performance is sorcery more seductive than ominous, more frightening than mysterious, more wicked than exquisite. But everyone who has passed once through the theater's cold iron gate and seen his magic becomes obsessed and returns every night thereafter. They themselves don't understand why they're so eager to go. My guess is that their very souls must become ensnared by his magic. But surely you won't be afraid of the magician. You, who prefer demons and monsters to humans, who live more in hallucinations than reality, will not be able to rest without seeing the acclaimed magician in the park. I, too, if I go with you, my love, will surely not be perplexed, however cruel the curses and spells invoked may be."

"And what's wrong with being perplexed, if the man is as beautiful as you say?" I laughed cheerfully, like a meadowlark singing in the fields of spring. In the next moment, however, betrayed by a faint malaise that rose in my breast and by a slight jealousy, I could not help but speak more forcefully. "All right, we'll go directly to the park. You and I will put him to the test—shall our souls be ensnared by his magic or not?"

We found ourselves wandering beside a huge fountain, on an avenue in the center of the city. A stone wall of milky marble encircled the fountain like a crown; statues of goddesses stood at intervals of six feet, and from below their feet springs gurgled and swelled, shooting water upward as if reaching for the stars in the firmament and, now forming rainbows, now clouds and mist in the glow of arc lights, burbled and sobbed in the night air. Sitting on a bench beneath the luxuriant foliage of roadside trees and gazing for a time at the swarms of people in the streets, we observed in the throng an extraordinary phenomenon. The four roads that converged from all sides of the city at a cross-way by the fountain were thronged with crowds enjoying an evening ramble, and almost everyone was streaming smoothly in the same direction. From the roads to the north, west, and east, walkers met at the plaza where the four roads crossed and then, forming an ever denser crowd, pressed into the road to the south in a thick black line. Resting on a bench beside the fountain, the two of us, quiet and solitary, were cut off from our surroundings like a floating island that has come to rest in the center of a great river.

"See how many people are drawn to the park. Let us go, too, quickly." Embracing my back gently, she rose. We joined the crowd with our arms locked firmly together, like links in a steel chain, so that we should not be separated however much we might be jostled.

For a time I advanced willy-nilly into the cloud of numberless people. When I looked ahead, the park appeared to be fairly close at hand, for green, red, yellow, and purple beams of dazzling electric light blazed so near the ground that they burned into the visitors' heads. Three- and four-story buildings that could have been brothels or restaurants lined the street on both sides; and when I looked up at their balconies, decorated with gaily illustrated paper lanterns that were strung like coral hair ornaments, drunken guests, both men and women, raged like wild beasts, indulging in every sort of outrageous behavior. Some looked down at the crowds in the street, showering abuse, telling jokes, and even spitting. Forgetting appearances and shame, they frolicked until a man made limp as jelly by his rampage, or a woman with hair as wild as a frenzied Asura's, would plunge from the balcony rail into the crowd. Instantly the mob would tear at their faces and rip off their clothing; and they would be borne away, one screaming, another as still as a corpse, like seaweed floating on the surf. I watched as one man who had fallen in front of me was carried off, upside down, with his legs sticking up like posts. First his shoes were removed by rogues who appeared from all directions, then his trousers were torn off, and finally his stockings, as he was pummeled and pinched. Then I observed a woman, bloated with drink, being hauled away, to the accompaniment of rhythmic shouts, in the same face-up position as the women in Giovanni Segantini's painting *The Punishment of Lust*.

Turning to my lover, I said, "The people in this city all seem to have taken leave of their senses. Is there a festival of some kind today?"

"But it's not only today. The people who come to the park enjoy themselves this way all year. They're always drunk like this. You and I are the only sober ones on the avenue."

She spoke quietly, as always, in graceful, earnest tones. Never losing her irresistible, inbred composure or her chaste passion, even in the most tumultuous scene or the most chaotic situation, she struck me as clean and noble, like a solitary goddess surrounded by a gang of devils. When I looked into her limpid eyes, I could only compare them to a mirrorlike autumnal sky, serenely clear in the midst of a raging storm.

Buffeted by waves of people, the two of us inched toward the park entrance just ahead of us; it seemed to take us more than an hour to arrive there. The people who had thronged together in dense profusion and crept along like a gigantic centipede broke into small groups when they finally reached the plaza inside the gates and scattered toward their various destinations. It may have been a park, but there were no hills or forests as far as the eye could see: as in a fairyland city, magnificent, lofty buildings in bizarre shapes, representing the ultimate in human accomplishment, soared in endless rows, burning millions of lights. Standing dazed in the center of the square, gazing around me at this thrilling spectacle, I was stupefied above all by an electric advertisement reading "Grand Circus" shining midway in the sky. The words appeared at the hub of what looked like a colossal Ferris wheel dozens of feet in diameter. Light bulbs covering the scores of spokes emitted refulgent shafts of light, formed a circle in space, as though someone had opened a giant's painted parasol, and continuously revolved, grandly and serenely. Even more astonishing, however, were the hundreds of acrobats, both men and women, wearing silky gauze against their bare skin, who scrambled up the brightly blazing columns and jumped unceasingly from upper to lower spokes as the wheel turned. Seen from a distance, these humans, dangling like bells everywhere on the wheel, glided in the luminous night sky, waving their garments buoyantly, like showering grains of light or dancing angels.

It was not only the wheel that caught my attention but also the weird, comical, and resplendent creations in light that writhed, flashed, and wriggled in almost every part of the sky over the park, like perpetual fireworks. If I were to show that celestial display to the citizens of Tokyo who delight in pyrotechnics on the river at Ryōgoku, or to the residents who marvel at the Daimonji bonfires on the mountains of Kyoto, how astonished they would be. Even in my brief survey at the time, I saw innumerable lines and designs, so intricate and bold that I remember them even now. Perhaps I could describe them by comparing them to the willful doodles of some demon equipped with superhuman, godly powers. Or I could say that they resembled the sun laughing, the moon weeping, and comets going berserk upon hearing that doomsday, the day of final judgment, was imminent, and all sorts of goblin stars trailed endlessly in every direction, to the farthest reaches of the heavens.

The plaza in which we stood formed a perfect half circle, and from the arc around it seven streets opened in all directions, like the ribs of a folding fan. The widest and most splendid of the seven was the avenue in the center. Of the hundreds of attractions in the park, most of the especially popular establishments seemed to be here, for every type of architecture—imposing, unstable, wild, symmetrical—was lined up like a fortress in an irregular jumble of different sizes. There was a buddhist temple in the style of the Golden Pavilion of Japan, a tall, Saracenic pavilion, and an eccentric tower that leaned even more than the one at Pisa, not to mention a monstrous, cup-shaped hall that grew fatter as it rose, a building in the shape of a human face, a roof crumpled like wastepaper, pillars as twisted as octopus legs, pounding waves, swirling maelstroms, warped structures, recurvate structures—the avenue delighted in multifarious shapes, some flat on the ground, some scraping the heavens.

"Sweetheart?"

My dear lover spoke and pulled at my sleeve.

"What are you staring at? You've come to this park often before, haven't you?"

"Any number of times," I said with a flustered nod, knowing that I should feel humiliated otherwise. "But I can't help staring each time I come. That's how much I love this park."

"Well, now," she said with an ingenuous smile. "The magician's theater is down there. Let's go quickly." Raising her left hand, she pointed to the end of the avenue.

At the spot where the plaza opened onto the avenue, a red de-mon's head, as large as the Great Buddha at Kamakura, glared at us. Emerald green lights flashed in the demon's eyes; sawlike teeth were exposed in a grin. The space between the upper and lower jaws, where the teeth sprouted, formed an arch through which many peo-ple were entering. As if that were not enough, the entire park glowed as brightly as a blast furnace, but this avenue was even brighter, and the force of the lights from the entire avenue gushed fiercely from the demon's mouth. When I plunged into the light, urged on by my lover, I felt as though my body should be consumed in flames.

Seen up close, the show venues lining both sides of the street like teeth on a comb were ostentatious, vulgar, and capricious. Motion picture posters, depicting with abandon the most preposterous scenes in garish pigments; the smell of paint, violently slopped on every building in peculiar, unspeakably disagreeable colors; the cha-os and debauchery of flags, banners, puppets, bands, and masquer-ade processions designed to draw customers—if I were to describe each of them in detail, my readers would cover their eyes in horror. To describe in a word my impression at the time, I would say the place presented a bizarre blend of beauty and ugliness, like the face of a nubile maiden disfigured by a festering growth, dripping with pus. Irregularity, comicality, and offensiveness were woven together, as if I were viewing the world of regular forms—the straight, the spherical, the flat—reflected in convex and concave mirrors. To be honest, I felt such fathomless terror and agitation as I walked that I thought more than once of turning back.

Had she not been with me, I might well have fled midway. As my heart grew increasingly timid, she moved ahead vigorously and light-heartedly, with the ingenuous steps of a child. Whenever I turned my cowed, pusillanimous eyes and gave her a pleading glance, she was wearing a delighted, innocent smile.

"How can an honest, gentle young woman like you view this ter-rifying scene with such composure?" Again and again I was on the point of asking her this, but I hesitated. If I had actually posed the question, how would she have replied? Would she say, "My composure is due to your influence"? Would she say, "It's because I have you, my love. For one who has entered the blind path of love, there is neither fear nor shame"? Yes. Without question, she would respond with these words. That is how ardently she trusts me, how genuinely she loves me. That this woman, mild as a sheep and pure as snow, takes delight in the park is evidence of her love for me. It is the result of her striving to adopt my interests as her own, my tastes as her own tastes. Some may say she has grown degenerate because of me. But however near her interests and tastes had drawn to the satanic, her mind and heart still retained human kindness and dignity.

With that in mind, I had to express my gratitude to her. It made me feel terribly inadequate to think that an apathetic man like me, who simply exists wearily and miserably, roaming from country to country embracing beautiful dreams, had mastered the spirit of a splendid young woman.

"I have no right to be the lover of a gentle woman like you. You're too noble, too upright a person to come to this park with me. I must warn you. For your sake, it would be infinitely better to break off our relationship. That you've become such a daring woman that you can walk calmly in a place like this makes me feel the horror of my crime."

Blurting this out, I stopped in the street, holding both her hands; but calm as always, she just smiled happily. Like a child unaware of how close she has drawn to the brink of destruction, she opened her bright eyes wide and gave me a refreshing, cheerful look.

After I had repeated myself several times, she said, "I'm ready. I understand without hearing it from you. I feel so happy, so fortunate, at this moment, to be walking with you down this street. If you feel sorry for me, I beg of you not to abandon me. Please don't doubt me, just as I don't doubt you." She spoke lightly, in the blithe, clear voice of a little bird. Then she urged me on again until we arrived before the magician's theater, where she said, "Now, my dear, we will put it to the test: which is stronger—our love or the magician's art?

I'm not the slightest bit afraid because I believe firmly in myself."
Again and again, she spurred me on.

I could not fail to be inspired by the consummate beauty of her devotion, however contemptible and depraved a person I may have been. "I was wrong to say what I did. It must be fate that a purehearted woman like you is tied to a sullied man like me. Our bodies and souls must have been linked in a previous life by the chains of an invisible bond. The karmic law of cause and effect dictates that you and I—a purehearted woman and a foul man—shall love each other forever. I'll lead you to the most mysterious, the most appalling hell, to say nothing of the magician. What do I have to fear if you say that you are not afraid?"

With these words, I knelt before her and gave the hem of her divine white robe a lingering kiss.

The magician's theater was located, as she had said, in a desolate area on the edge of a bustling district. Emerging suddenly from a seething, strepitous quarter into this dim, gloomy space, my nerves, far from settling, were seized by an even greater eeriness and sensed a gathering apprehension, as if an unforeseen disaster awaited me. Until now I had thought it odd that the park completely lacked any natural beauty—no trees, forests, or water—but arriving in this area, I saw that these elements had been put to use here. The natural features employed here had not, of course, been arranged to reproduce a natural scene; rather, they had been used as material for promoting artificiality and supplementing the effects of warped craftsmanship. Seeing these words, some readers may picture the gardening arts depicted in such stories as Poe's "The Domain of Arnheim" or "Landor's Cottage," but the man-made landscape of which I speak seemed to employ even more elaborate handiwork and to be farther removed from natural scenery than those. In short, trees, plants, and water were manipulated as devices for bringing buildings to completion, just as arches, signs, and lighting are used. It might be best to call it architecture that took the form of a landscape rather than a miniaturized or improved nature. Equipped with forests and groves that lacked the vigorous life force one expects in vegetation, and full of just-right lines that resembled clever replicas, the scene gave the impression more of a stage set than a garden. Leaves had simply been used instead of paint, water instead of wave curtains, and hillocks instead of papier-mâché.[5]

If I were to evaluate this scenery as a set, I would say that it formed a distinctive, lurid scene, capturing something of natural beauty that is difficult to attain. Every branch of each tree and the shape of each stone were arranged so as to hold a suggestion of melancholy and expressed a recondite concept, to the extent that we forgot we were looking at trees and rocks and instead felt intimations of terror. Readers are probably familiar with Böcklin's painting *The Isle of the Dead*. The scene I am trying to describe produced an effect somewhat resembling that of the painting, but it was achieved with objects even colder, darker, and more forlorn than Böcklin's. What unsettled my nerves most of all was a towering black grove of poplars that encircled the space like a folding screen. It took me a long time to realize that it was a grove because, seen from a distance, it presented an appearance so inscrutable that one could hardly believe it was a grove. A pitch-black, flat barrier, just like a prison wall, lacking both head and feet, formed a circle like a well curb and soared to the sky. Moreover, when I scrutinized it more closely, I saw that this sinuous circumvallation took the form of two gigantic bats standing apart at the right and left but spreading wide their black wings and clutching each other's paws. The more carefully I looked, the more vividly the bats' eyes, ears, paws, and the gaps between their wings filled the space between heaven and earth, like a crisp shadow cast against shoji. Thus is it not surprising that I struggled to determine what this ingenious silhouette was made of. The monster had first looked like a forest, then like a wall, and then like bats; and when

---

5. Paint, wave curtains, and papier-mâché are materials commonly used on the kabuki stage. A wave curtain is a large canvas painted with waves used in scenes on or near a body of water.

it turned out to be a dense clump of luxuriant aspens, shaped with subtle art to mimic on a grand scale the form of two beasts, I could not help but feel even greater astonishment and admiration.

"You don't know who designed this forest, do you? The magician made it. Recently, on his own initiative, he directed gardeners to haul in large trees and plant them in a very short time. Not one of the men who undertook this work realized what shape the forest would take. They simply planted the trees, one by one, as the magician commanded. When the forest was completed, the magician smiled happily and cried, 'Forest, oh forest! Assume the shape of bats and strike terror into the human heart!' As he spoke, he raised his magic staff and hit the ground three times. Instantly, the workers who stood there perceived that the aspen forest they had planted in a daze resembled the shadow of some monstrous bird. After that the magician's fame spread throughout the city, along with the story of the forest. Some say that the forest isn't shaped like a monstrous bird but that viewers embrace that illusion. In any case, everyone who passes here on the way to the magician's theater is alarmed by the shadow and feels his blood run cold. Is the forest bewitched or are the viewers? Only the magician himself knows the secret."

As I listened to her tale, I examined the scene still more closely.

The magic forest—this is what the residents of the city called it—not only was shaped like a monster but also served an essential function by forming a circle of dark banners, towering in the sky, which effectively screened the enclosed area from the bright colors of the rest of the park and created a desolate scene abounding in darkness and spells. The enclosed area must have been about the size of Shinobazu Pond.[6] A foul, stagnant, dank marsh, emitting a cold sheen like that of ice, appeared to extend over most of the space. I had doubted my eyes when I saw the magic forest, and now, facing this marsh, I hesitated to judge whether its wonderfully still

---

6. Shinobazu Pond, in the Ueno district of Tokyo, has a circumference of about 1.25 miles (2 kilometers).

surface was in fact water or a sheet of glass. Indeed, the frost-white water seemed so inert and congealed that one could almost believe it was a sheet of glass and that a stone thrown into it would rebound with a clatter. In the center of this marsh, as alone and forbidding as Death, floated a sort of promontory, which might have been an island or a boat, on the pointed summit of which burned pale blue lights spelling out "The Kingdom of Magic," like a solitary star illuminating the eternal darkness of night.

I must explain in more detail what the "sort of promontory" was. It was a towering mass of rocks that closely resembled the Mountain of Needles depicted in paintings of hell. It crouched there silently, a heap of triangular boulders as sharp as halberds, lacking any plants, trees, or houses. From this alone, even with a sign announcing "The Kingdom of Magic," it was impossible to tell where the kingdom might be.

"Over there. There's the entrance to the magician's theater." Sure enough, in the direction she pointed, wedged between two boulders near the sign, was what appeared to be a small, narrow iron gate. A makeshift bridge extended from where we stood, at the edge of the marsh, to the gate.

"But the gate looks firmly shut. There don't seem to be any spectators going in, and I don't hear any voices. Is he performing his magic, even so?" I spoke as if to myself.

"Yes," she said immediately, with a nod. "He's probably just beginning. Unlike the usual trickster, I've heard that this magician doesn't use music or invite applause during his performance. That's how intense and brisk the magic is, they say. Holding their breath, the people in the audience feel almost as if they've been drenched in cold water and do nothing but emit quiet sighs. Judging from the silence of the place, I'd say they must be in the midst of a performance right now." Perhaps because of an irrepressible terror, or perhaps a strange excitement, her voice rasped and quavered uncharacteristically.

Saying nothing further, we started across the makeshift bridge toward the island.

Entering the gate, I had taken only five or six steps when blinding rays of light, filling the room, suddenly paralyzed my eyes—accustomed to a world of ghastly darkness—and caused as much pain as if those eyes were being gouged by a drill. The Kingdom of Magic, the exterior of which had looked like a towering clod of earth, turned out to encompass a huge, glittering, gold-plated theater. Magnificent decorations, adorning every inch of the columns and ceilings and mirroring the effulgent lights, shone in my wakening eyes. The place was filled to capacity, every seat in the parterre, second floor, and third floor so packed that one could hardly move. The audience included every costume and every race—Chinese, Indian, European—but for some reason I saw no one except the two of us wearing Japanese clothes. In special boxes, a resplendent group of gentlemen and ladies from the city's high society—people who would not be expected to set foot casually in the park—sat in rows. One of these ladies covered her face like a Muslim woman and hunched in the shadows, as if fearing what others of good birth might say; but in her eyes as they took in the stage, fresh, vivid hues of elegance and passion betrayed her secret. Among the gentlemen were some whose names were known in various fields—great statesmen of the country, business tycoons, artists, religious leaders, playboys. I had the feeling I had already seen many of their faces, time and again, in photographs. One of them looked like Napoleon, another like Bismarck; one had features like Dante's, one like Byron's. Perhaps Nero and Socrates were there, too, and Goethe and Don Juan. I understood immediately why they had come to this kingdom of devils. Sages, despots, poets, and scholars alike possess hearts that are drawn to the "mysterious." They would probably say that they had come for research, for the experience, or to proselytize. Perhaps they believe so themselves. But if you ask me, in the depths of their souls lurks a nature that, in varying degrees, feels beauty as I feel it and dreams the same dreams I do. The only difference is that, unlike me, they are unaware of the beauty and the dreams, or do not affirm them. —Such were my random thoughts.

Making our way through the parterre seating, where Chinese queues, African turbans, and ladies' bonnets mingled like waves of red and white lotus blossoms, she and I were finally able to secure two seats. Between us and the stage stood at least five or six rows, most of whose places were occupied by young European ladies turned out in smart, early-summer fashions, their plump, clean necks aligned, sitting like a brood of swans. My gaze passed over the many strata of women's shoulders to focus on the stage beyond them.

A single black curtain covered the back of the stage. In the center, on the highest dais, stood a splendid throne—the seat, no doubt, of the king of this Kingdom of Magic. There the magician sat erect, extremely youthful, a crown of living snakes on his head, a Roman toga draped on his body, and golden sandals on his feet. Below the dais, to the right and left of the throne, three male and three female assistants knelt formally like slaves, kowtowing respectfully, the soles of their feet toward the audience. There were no other sets or people on the stage; it was exceedingly simple.

From my coat pocket I extracted the program I had received at the entrance. Opening it, I saw a list of twenty or thirty acts, each of them, I imagined, unprecedented and astounding. If I were to mention two or three that particularly fanned my curiosity, the first would be something called *mesmerism*. According to the brief explanation provided by the program, the magician would induce sleep in the entire audience, and everyone present would experience an illusion in accordance with a hint the magician provided. For example, if the magician said, "It is now five o'clock in the morning," everyone would see the bracing rays of the morning sun and find that his pocket watch showed five o'clock. Or, if he said, "This is a field," a field would appear; if "The sea," an ocean would appear; if "Rain," everyone's body would be drenched. The next most amazing act was called "The Contraction of Time." In this the magician would sow a seed in a bit of soil and calmly chant a spell, whereupon in the space of ten minutes the seed would sprout, produce a stem, blossom, and fruit. Moreover, not only would he ask members of the audience to provide the seed, selected from anywhere they wished, but also, without fail, he would raise even the tallest trunk, surpassing the clouds, or produce the densest foliage, filling the sky, within ten minutes. Similar, but even more uncanny, was an act entitled "Mysterious Pregnancy." In this case, too, according to the program, the magician would induce pregnancy in a woman through the power of a spell and cause her to give birth, all within ten minutes. The woman employed for this magic was usually a slave of the "kingdom," but the program stated that volunteers from the audience were especially welcome. These examples should be enough for the reader to understand that the magician belonged to a different class than the commonplace trickster.

Unfortunately, most of the program had been completed by the time I entered the theater: only the last act remained. As soon as we had reached our seats, the magician rose deliberately from his throne, stepped to the front of the stage, and, blushing like a child, set about explaining the next magic act in a charming, shy, quiet voice.

"Now then, for tonight's last act, I will introduce you to the most engrossing, the most incomprehensible magic. For now let's call it 'The Art of Human Metamorphosis.' In short, through the power of my spells, this technique shall instantly transform any human body into any other object you desire—whether a bird, a bug, an animal, or inanimate matter, including liquids such as water or liquor. Or, it can also limit the transformation to a specific part of the body—the head, for example, or the feet, the shoulders, the buttocks . . ."

Enthralled less by his fluid speech than by his charming features and graceful figure, I could not help staring at him spellbound as he patiently continued his narrative. I had heard that he was blessed with extraordinary beauty, but now, comparing his actual appearance to the face I had imagined on the basis of rumors, I realized that there was a marked difference in the degree of beauty. What surprised me most is that one could not distinguish whether this magician, whom I had thought of all along as a very young man, was male or female. A woman would probably have said he was a peerlessly beautiful man, but a man might have said that this was a woman of unprecedented beauty. I perceived that the masculine refinement, wisdom, and vigor of his physique, his musculature, his bearing, and his voice blended harmoniously with feminine grace, delicacy, and cunning. The subtle balance in every detail—for example, the abundant chestnut hair; the full cheeks in a plump, oval face; the red lips; the elegant yet virile shape of the hands and feet—resembled the constitution of an adolescent boy or girl in whom sexual traits are not yet fully developed. Another mystery in his outward appearance was the matter of race and country of origin. This is a question that would naturally occur to anyone who saw the color of his skin: this man—or woman?—was neither purely white nor Mongoloid nor black. If I were forced to come up with a parallel, I might say that his features and physique bore some resemblance to the tribes of the Caucasus, a place said to produce the most beautiful people in the world. A more apt description, however, would be to say that he was a racial mix of the most complex kind, his body consisting entirely of the strong points and virtues of every race, and that he was the most complete representation of human beauty. Holding an exotic appeal for everyone, he was qualified to attempt the sexual seduction of men and women alike, and to captivate their hearts.

". . . Now, I would like to ask all of you for your help," the magician continued. "First, as a demonstration, I will transform each of the six slaves who kneel here in attendance. But to prove how mysterious, how miraculous my magic is, I hope that you, ladies and gentlemen of the audience, will bestir yourselves to submit to my magic. More than two months have passed since I began to perform in this park, and every night during that time many volunteers from the audience have ascended the stage for my sake and docilely sacrificed themselves to magic. Sacrificed . . . that's right. This is a sacrifice. No one will come to the stage who lacks the courage to shame himself, in plain sight of everyone, by allowing his precious human shape to be manipulated by my powers and turned into a dog, a pig, a stone, or a heap of soil rich with manure. Nevertheless, every night I have been able to find in these seats any number of praiseworthy sacrificial victims. I've heard that highborn, aristocratic men and women, too, have secretly joined the ranks of victims. Accordingly, I believe—indeed, I am proud—that many volunteers will come forward tonight, too, as every night."

When the magician had said this, a ghastly, triumphant smile rose to his pallid face. Further, it seemed that the more the members of the audience listened to his audacious speech and observed his overbearing manner, the more they felt their souls being drawn to him and subjugated by him.

Finally the magician beckoned to a sweet, tender beauty from among the slaves who knelt before the throne, looking like a group of statues with their hands and foreheads pressed to the floor. Like a somnambulist, she tottered up to him, fell again to her knees, and let her head fall limply, like a marionette whose strings have slackened.

"You, of all my slaves, are the most charming girl, the girl I like best. If you persevere another five or six years, I will make a splendid magician of you. I will make you the leading magician in the world, unmatched by humans, gods, or devils. I'm sure you consider it your great happiness to have become my follower. No doubt you have recognized that it is a far more happy thing to be a slave in the kingdom of devils than to be a queen in the world of humans." The magician stood upright, his shoulders thrown back, as he solemnly uttered these words and spread her long hair on the floor with his foot. "Now I will perform the Art of Metamorphosis. What do you wish to become tonight? As you know, I'm a deeply compassionate king. I'll make you into anything you want. Tell me what you'd like." His tone of voice suggested that he was granting her a delightful favor.

At that moment her entire body, which had been as stiff as plaster of paris, suddenly began to twitch and shake, as if she had felt an electric shock, and her lips began to move, like water in a thawing river. "Thank you, Your Majesty. I wish to become a peacock and fly in a circle above your throne." Like a Brahmin fakir in prayer, she raised her hands high in the air, palms pressed together.

With a cheerful nod, the magician began to recite a spell under his breath. He had spoken of ten minutes, but in less than five the woman's torso and limbs were covered with peacock feathers. In the remaining five minutes, the human elements from the shoulders up gradually turned into a peacock head. At the start of these five minutes, the peacock, which still possessed the head of a young woman, raised its joyful eyes and smiled, then closed its eyes in a trance and drew its eyebrows together, and slowly the head changed into the head of a wretched bird. This process seemed to me the most poetic sight of all. At the end of ten minutes, the woman, now completely transformed into a peacock, flew up with a smart clap of beating wings, circled the ceiling above the audience two or three times, then flew back toward the throne, quietly descended to the middle step of the dais like a brocade cloud sinking to the ground, and quickly spread its tail wide, as if opening a painted fan.

The remaining five slaves were summoned, one by one, before the king, who quickly administered his magic. One of the three men said he wished to become a leopard skin and be spread under the king's throne. The other two said they would become candle stands of pure silver and illuminate the dais from the right and the left. Finally, the remaining female slaves said they wanted to change into two gentle butterflies and cling lightly to the king's body. These five requests were immediately granted.

The audience that had assembled in the theater to witness these unheard-of feats were struck dumb with shock and, doubting their sense of sight, could only look on in astonishment. In particular, when the first male slave was struck by the magician's staff, he grew as thin as a cracker and finally turned into a beautiful leopard skin. At that very moment we heard a painful moan, and I saw the woman who sat in front of me cover her face in horror and cling to her male companion.

"Well, ladies and gentlemen, . . . does anyone wish to become a sacrificial victim?" With a look even more exultant than before, the magician chased back and forth on the stage, following the two butterflies fluttering about him. ". . . Is the idea of becoming a captive in the kingdom of devils so revolting to you all? Do you believe that human dignity and the human form are so precious that you must cling to them? Perhaps you think the lot of the slaves who have been transformed for my sake is wretched, pitiable. But even if their outward appearance be that of butterflies, a peacock, a leopard skin, or candle stands, they have not lost their human emotions and sensibilities. And their breasts overflow with a limitless joy and rapture, such as you have never experienced in your dreams. Anyone who has sampled my magic once will surely know what happiness they are feeling . . ."

When the magician's eyes swept the inside of the theater, all the men and women hunched their shoulders and hid their faces in their laps, perhaps fearing that they would be hypnotized by his glare. Suddenly, a rustle of silk and the faint echo of a lady's shoes, walking toward the stage from a corner of the parterre, broke the deep silence.

"Magician! You remember me, I'm sure. Captivated more by your beauty than by your magic, I came both yesterday and today to watch. If you will include me among your sacrifices, I shall be satisfied that my love has been fulfilled. Please make me into the golden sandals you wear on your feet."

Drawn by this voice, I fearfully lifted my face and saw the lady I had noticed earlier, seated in a special box with her face covered, now prostrating herself like a martyr before the magician.

Bewitched by the magician's charm, dozens of men and women followed the veiled lady unsteadily to the stage. The twentieth person to leave his seat in a trance, with the aim of becoming a sacrificial victim, was none other than me.

Clutching my sleeve, my lover spoke, tears streaming down her face. "Alas, you have surrendered to the magician after all. My love for you has not wavered in the face of the magician's beauty, but you have been seduced by him and forgotten me. You're about to abandon me to serve the magician. What a spineless, fickle person you are!"

"As you say, I am spineless. Infatuated with the magician's beauty, I forgot all about you. Yes, I have surrendered. But there's something more important to me than winning or surrendering." Even as I spoke, my soul was being drawn toward the magician, as a scrap of iron is attracted to a magnet.

I ran up onto the stage. "Magician! I want to be a faun," I raved. "I want to become a faun and dance wildly before your throne. Please grant my wish and use me as your slave."

"All right. Your wish is very appropriate for you. There was no need for you to be born as a human being in the first place."

With a great laugh, the magician struck me once on the back with his magic staff. Thick wool immediately began to grow on both legs, and two horns appeared on my head. Simultaneously, in my breast, the agony of human conscience disappeared completely, and a joy as bright as the sun and as wide as the sea gushed forth inexhaustibly.

In my joy, I frolicked rapturously around the stage for a moment; but soon my former lover interrupted my pleasure.

Following my steps, she rushed onto the stage and spoke to the magician. "I've come here not because I have been ensnared by your beauty or your magic. I've come to take back my lover. Please be good enough to change that repulsive faun back into a man and return him to me immediately. Or, if you say you cannot do so, then transform me into the same shape. Even though he has abandoned me, I can never abandon him. If he has become a faun, then I will become a faun as well. I will accompany him to the end, wherever he may go."

"All right, then, I'll make you into a faun, too."

With these words from the magician, she changed in an instant into a hideous, accursed half beast. Then she ran at me headlong and abruptly locked her horns firmly with mine. No matter how our heads danced and leaped, we had become inseparable.

RED ROOFS

Translated by Anthony H. Chambers

1

Mayuko alighted from a streetcar at Nakayamate Sanchōme, spontaneously assumed a pose, and began to walk down the asphalt road that leads straight to Sannomiya. A spring came into her step.

The weather is beautiful, and my ring should be ready by noon—She had come into Kobe on an impulse, suddenly wanting to see the ring. She enjoyed walking smartly along this street, even if it took her out of her way. The slope, which the locals call Tor Road, was the most agreeable spot in the beautiful city of Kobe, most of whose streets were hardened with asphalt. Behind her rose the hill on which stands the Tor Hotel, cloaked in fresh green foliage; and from there the road descended toward the shore in a straight line so sharply defined that it might have been drawn in chalk. In the distance, toward the coastline, tall structures stood conspicuously under the clear blue sky of May, like stacks of sugar cubes—the Meikai Building, the Oriental Hotel. Walking down this street, Mayuko always recalled the avenues of Shanghai, where she had spent a year, and felt as though she were living in Shanghai even now.

The pavement flattened under the rubber soles of her athletic shoes as she trod, silently and firmly, with the step of a drill horse, on her quiet way down the slope; here and there, shop windows on both sides of the street reflected her bright yellow outfit, fluttering like a butterfly.—A one-piece dress of artificial silk, which she had just knitted herself; a hand-knit scarf of the same fabric, wrapped once under her chin with the rest draping behind; no flowers or ribbons; and a hat of thick wool, in the same color: aside from her shoes, stockings, and patent-leather belt, her clothing was entirely yellow and revealed a taste for simplicity that was surprising in a woman of her profession. Knowing that her skin, pale in the Spanish manner, was set off nicely by these crude handmade garments, she sometimes tried them on when she thought of going for a walk; and today, as she left the house, she had been too lazy to put on a corset. Under the dress, only a soft chemise wrapped part of her torso, and the breeze striking her bare skin through the loose, silk weave as she walked gave her the buoyant sensation of being naked. Striding along in these clothes and brandishing a rattan cane equipped with a leather strap, she might have been mistaken from a distance for a Western typist taking exercise during her lunch break. Hoping to be seen in this way, in fact, she wore her hat so low when she walked down this street that only her lips, coated with French rouge, and the upturned tip of her nose stood out beneath the brim.

"Have you finished the repairs?" She stepped into Swan & Company on her way down the slope and addressed the head clerk. Squirming like a fretful child, she grasped her cane in both hands and bounced it against her knees.

"Let's see, Miss Miyajima. I think . . ."

"You promised it by noon today, without fail, so it must be ready. Look, it's already past two o'clock."

A tiny watch glittered on her wrist; she thrust it at the clerk's nose.

"Ah, yes, I think it's ready. I'll just take a look."

While the clerk was in the back room, she paced back and forth impatiently, scrutinizing each jewel on the shelves as if looking for something appealing. "Here," she would call to the shop assistant, gazing at a stone she had picked up. "What's this?" At such moments, could life be more carefree and delightful for this young lady of leisure?

The item for which she had ordered repairs was an aquamarine ring she had spotted in the window five or six days before and decided to buy at once; but, displeased with the reddishness of the gold setting, she had directed the shop to make the gold more yellow. She wanted a color that would go well with the hand-knit dress she wore today and with an organdy summer dress she had ordered. Besides, she thought, that reddish gold would be a poor match for the gold of her wristwatch.

"Why, this is no better at all." Opening the velvet box the head clerk had given her, she scowled crossly.

"Yes, miss. No, . . . it has been fixed . . ."

"It has not! It's still reddish brown! Look!" She plucked the ring from the box and held it up to her dress. "See? The dress is much more yellow. I asked you the other day to make the ring the same color. What's wrong with you?"

"I see what you mean—there is still a touch of red, but not enough to clash with your dress."

"No, I won't have it! How could I wear such a thing?"

Mayuko found herself in a dilemma at times like this. Though she was fussy about color combinations and fabric quality, she wanted to put on something as soon as she bought it—she would not be satisfied until she paraded it before everyone that very day—and because of this impetuousness, she might, for example, make all sorts of demands at a fitting; but after three or four alterations, her desire for the garment would prevail and she would tell herself, *It'll do, it's too much trouble, put up with it.* Merchants laughed at her, and she herself would come out a loser.

"Here! What can you do about it? Can't you make it more yellow?"

"Yes, we can. In that case I'll send it back to the factory again."

"When will it be ready? I don't know what you're thinking, but I'm a Tokyo girl. I can't stand the way people here in western Japan take their time about things."

The clerk laughed politely. "You needn't worry about that. I'll have the work done right away. Please be patient for another five or six days."

"Five or six days?"

"That's right, how about Wednesday next week? There'll be no mistake this time."

The ring lay in her hand. Reluctant to let it go, she rolled it around on her palm a few times, then put it on her little finger and turned the back of her hand toward the light.

"What do you think? Maybe it's not so bad?"

"It's not bad at all, Miss, and the gold is much yellower than it was before."

"How about compared to this watch? Doesn't it look different?"

There was no point in asking the clerk, but she persevered until she was satisfied.

"All right," she said, "I'll let you have this round." She sounded uncomfortable, having been so overbearing before. Putting the empty box in her pocket, she made no move to take the ring off her little finger.

"Good-bye. I'll come again in four or five days. If you see some earrings with nice stones, set them aside for me."

Returning to the street, she glanced anxiously at the "yellow" of her ring as she walked. *I only have a ten-yen note with me, but Odagiri will be coming tonight, and he's sure to give me one or two hundred. I'll be rich again tomorrow, so perhaps I'll take a turn through Motomachi now and look for something to buy. Lane Crawford and Rhea probably have new summer clothes. And pretty soon I'll need to buy something to wear at the beach this year . . .*

Crossing the tracks at Sannomiya and coming to the streetcar line, she stopped, asked herself again if she wanted to go to Motomachi, and looked at her wristwatch. It was exactly three o'clock. *Odagiri will probably come at seven or eight in the evening, and there will be nothing to do at home if I go back now. But then a reply might have come from Teramoto. He always answers quickly; his letter is likely to come in today's afternoon mail. A square, Western-style envelope of heavy, cloth-patterned paper. On it, "Miss Miyajima Mayuko," in characters as thick, skillful, firm, and masculine as if they'd been written with a brush . . .* His handwriting, in the rich ink of a fountain pen, danced before her eyes. She pictured his hand grasping the fountain pen. A hand bronzed by the sun. A hand sturdy as a rock, with strong bones and callouses on all five fingers from playing catch. Mayuko loved those hands. How happy she would be if they would grasp her and hug her so tightly that her bones would splinter, so tightly that her life would end. *I've never seen his body, since he always wears a university uniform, but surely he has a splendid physique to go with those hands. A supple, powerful torso with black hair on his chest. Full, muscular shoulders, like a boxer's. Strong arms, deep breaths . . . All of him, surely, brimming with inexhaustible youth and purity, the very picture of health . . .*

"I don't have money today; I'd better go home and read his letter." She had taken two or three steps toward Motomachi, but, reconsidering, she turned back. When she reached Lane Crawford's, she did pause to peer at the window display, but soon she crossed the street and sat in Juchheim's for five minutes while she sipped a cup of black tea and ate three or four Western-style pastries; then she boarded a streetcar bound for Kamitsutsui.

2

Mayuko's house was between Osaka and Kobe, near a little stop on the Takarazuka line, which branched off from the main line of the Hankyū Electric Railroad at Nishinomiya Station. Seen from the train, the whitish soil was as bright as a sandy beach; a wide, shallow river trickled through an unbroken forest of charming little pines. Mayuko, who disliked all things gloomy and wished to live gaily and brightly, had admired the view here when she first came to look for a house. The clean-washed color of the earth was a novelty to her eyes, accustomed as they were to the dark soil of the Tokyo suburbs. Not only was the ground white but also the sand in the riverbed, the stones reinforcing the banks, and the walls of the Culture Homes that stood sparsely here and there. The monochrome was interrupted only by the red roof tiles on the houses, the red trunks of the pine trees, and the dark green of new foliage. As she surveyed the scene, the landscape formed by these three clear, basic colors was as fresh as if the oils had not yet dried on a painting, and the rays of the early summer sun reflected so strongly that they hurt her eyes.

It had been only a year since a developer had begun to manage this tract and named it the Suikōen Culture Village, but in the short time since Mayuko moved here, five or six new houses had already appeared on a hill in the middle distance and along the river nearby. The house she rented faced the river to the south and was enclosed by a few pines; the garden ended abruptly at a stone embankment below which the water flowed. The exterior of the house was in the Western style, but the interior was of Japanese design, with low ceilings, many partitions, and surprisingly poor air circulation: "With all these pines and the stream nearby, the summers are cool," the developer had said, but the reality was different; to an extent, Mayuko had been taken in by this sales pitch, and she had been persuaded to move in when she stepped inside the first time and found the tatami and everything else so new that the walls still smelled of fresh paint.

The second floor consisted of two rooms of eight and six mats, respectively [12 × 12 and 9 × 12 feet], with a continuous veranda outside; and downstairs, in addition to the bath and kitchen, there were three rooms plus an entry hall. Three people lived there: Mayuko, the mistress of the house; her cousin, O-miyo; and O-moto, a servant girl; but Odagiri came from time to time, the film processor Onchi had taken to sleeping over recently, and, if not Odagiri or Onchi, a man who worked at Mayuko's film studio would be there, or someone she knew from the cinema, or a dance partner, and so the house was never without signs of a man.

"It's hot! I wore a light dress today, but I worked up a sweat walking." Arriving home at about four o'clock, Mayuko flung her cane to the floor of the entryway with such a "bang" that the hard-packed cement seemed about to crack. She unbuckled her dusty shoes.

"Welcome home," O-miyo mumbled, almost inaudibly, coming out to the entryway. She was eighteen, five years younger than Mayuko, and did not resemble her cousin at all: she had been born with a hunchback and acted a bit too grown up for her face and body, which seemed to have stopped developing at the age of fourteen or fifteen. Her home in the Honjo district had burned down in the Great Earthquake two years before, and, after a period of hardship in Tokyo, she had been brought here to live with Mayuko, whom she referred to as her big sister; but the taciturn, high-strung, fastidious girl had taken charge of Mayuko's disorderly household and accomplished the work of three servants, becoming her cousin's devoted, priceless treasure. Odagiri, too, had said, "The poor child, you must look after her." He would give her pocket money, but O-miyo put it all aside with her wages until she had accumulated enough that Mayuko would say, "Miyo, do you have ten yen?" and end up borrowing from her. But O-miyo never frowned at these requests or asked to be repaid. "No, no, any time at all," she would say.

"Everybody in Kobe is wearing white slacks. I'll wear my flannels today. Would you get them out for me?" Stepping up into the house with one bare foot, Mayuko kicked off the other shoe, which landed upside down in the entryway. "All right," said O-miyo. She stepped down into the entry, picked up the shoes, and inserted shoe trees while Mayuko headed upstairs.

All the windows stood refreshingly open, and, perhaps because she had come in from the brightness outside, the peaceful darkness of the room soothed her flushed face, and reflections from the river imparted a subdued luster to everything—the majolica vase, the glass in the bookcase, the surface of the desk—like the sheen of quiet water. The only sounds were the faint chatter of birds, deep in the pine grove, and the murmur of flowing water. Though she had lived here less than six months, she already felt the tranquil satisfaction of returning to her own home. And then she stepped to the desk, where newly arrived mail would be lying.

"Miss Miyajima Mayuko"—the words, inscribed with a fountain pen, immediately caught her eye. The envelope was so sturdy it was difficult to tear; quickly cutting it open, she read as she stood.

I have just received your letter. Thank you for inviting me to visit this

Sunday afternoon. I would love to go, but unfortunately my father and sister are here from Hokkaido for sight-seeing in Kyoto, and so I regret that I cannot avail myself of your kindness. After they have returned home, let us arrange a convenient time for me to pay you a leisurely visit. I look forward to a splendid meal at that time. Forgive me for being selfish; I hope you will not think badly of me.

The other day Nanjing Romance *was playing in Kyōgoku. I had seen it once in Tokyo, but I went to see it again because I like you in that Chinese robe. I think your face in that picture is the most—no, I should not say that—is extremely beautiful. The Chinese gown is truly lovely. I did not think much of the picture itself, though.*

Until later, then. I hope I can see you soon. From what you have said I imagine that Suikōen is a very fine place, and so I will be honored if you show me where you live.

"Miyo!" After she had scanned it, she tossed the letter on the desk and shouted to the bottom of the stairs. "Miyo, did you get out my flannels? And I'm going to rinse off, so draw some water in the bathroom."

Undressing, she went down to the tiled bathroom, where she ran over phrases of the letter to herself as she scrubbed her body with a cold towel . . . "I will be honored if you show me where you live." . . . *His letters are always like that, and his manner too diffident, indecisive, never forthright.* "I think your face in that picture is . . . extremely beautiful. The Chinese gown is truly lovely. I did not think much of the picture itself, though." . . . *Then what about me, myself? Does he mean to say that he likes me in the picture but isn't interested in the real me? Who cares about a Chinese robe? He's not the type to use flattery or irony; he should just say what he thinks. He can't help it if his father and sister really have come to visit, but somehow it doesn't ring true. Is he on his guard against me, after all?* . . .

When Mayuko had washed off her white makeup and emerged refreshed from the bath, O-miyo was waiting with the flannels. Five inches shorter than Mayuko, she had to reach up to drape a dry towel softly over her cousin's shoulders. Then she wiped the last of the moisture from Mayuko's hips, which were dimpled on both sides, and from the rich flesh of her back.

Mayuko asked for a brimming cup of freshly drawn water, gulped it down, and stretched out on a rattan chaise longue on the second-floor veranda, enjoying the lingering warmth of her bath. Then she spread out the letter on her lap and reread it slowly.

Teramoto, the author of the letter, was a student in the Law Faculty of Kyoto University; she had not known him very long. When she had come to Kyoto after the earthquake and was living in Okazaki, there was a boardinghouse for students next door—or, more precisely, she had chosen to live next to the boardinghouse because she liked to make friends with young students; and before long she had seized some opportunity or other to approach them—to put it nicely, she did this spontaneously; to put it less flattering-ly, she was brazen—and would drop in at the boardinghouse or in-vite students to her place for tea. For their part, the students were amused and welcomed this tomboyish, rambunctious actress. Some of them would ask for tours of the temporary studio at Kurodani or tag along when she went on location. At the time, Teramoto lodged in Shimogamo and would sometimes drop in at the boardinghouse next door, where he was simply one of the group. As the others ex-changed jokes, he would always listen silently, with an expression that said, "What are they laughing at?" He did not seem to be affect-ed, nor was he shy, but somehow he looked ill at ease. At first Mayuko neither liked nor disliked the youth, but once she had said, "I want to learn to ride a horse," whereupon Teramoto had replied, "I'll be glad to teach you. I rode all the time when I lived in Hokkaido, and I'm comfortable on a horse." He escorted her to the riding grounds at Maruyama and Mibu. While she was learning from him, she realized at some point that the boy had a crush on her.

Mayuko had decided that most young men would gladly do things for her if she flirted with them a little, that they would not hesitate to serve her, and so Teramoto's kindness did not make a particularly strong impression; but she did think she might as well have a little fun with him if he was infatuated with her. The fact of his being a university student excited her curiosity as well. She had many acquaintances among students, but she had never carried on an affair with one. Gradually her heart was drawn to Teramoto and his student uniform. The feeling of his arms when he helped her on and off the horse with both hands—arms so hard that they might ring if struck with a piece of wood; his swelling chest, which threatened to send his brass buttons flying; his close-cropped head and round face; his buttocks, clearly outlined under his melton trousers. He was rather short in proportion to his torso, and he was on the wide side, somewhat like the fatso role in comedies; his legs were bent *O-Beine*—Teramoto himself had used the German term. "Miss Mayuko, your legs form an *X*, don't they? That's unusual for a Japanese person. Knock-kneed legs like yours are called *X-Beine*, and mine, which form an *O*, are called *O-Beine*," he had explained.—His was a rather ungainly physique, but Mayuko felt that she would love to run and crash into his body. As a woman who was attracted to slender men and prized good looks above all else, she sensed a novel freshness and cleanness in the face of this man, so like a common soldier, in whom only the straight teeth and clear eyes were white. For whatever reason, however, Teramoto seemed to flee whenever she tried to contrive an opportunity to be alone with him.

"Won't you take me on a long ride sometime?" They were riding along the Kamo riverbank.

"All right. Where do you want to go?"

"Someplace far. We could spend the night."

"That won't do; your legs would be sore the next day."

"Well, I could come back by train, couldn't I?"

"There's no need for that; you can go pretty far in a day trip."

Mayuko felt an odd constraint when she was with this man. Since he never relaxed his polite way of speaking, she, too, could not bring herself to use crudely direct language. *He must be a coward; he's in love with me, but he's afraid of what might happen; but it will happen, even if he is afraid; I'll show him, before long, if I just have a chance to spend a night with him* . . . She had derived a perverse pleasure from these secret thoughts, but presently she left Kyoto behind and moved to Suikōen, where she acquired new hangers-on, found companions nearby, and in her usual fickle way forgot about Teramoto without really meaning to.

It had been only a month before, when she went to Kyoto for a shoot, that she suddenly wanted to see Teramoto again. Finishing her part early, she was wandering idly along Kyōgoku and thought of calling Teramoto. When she telephoned from the Café Royal, he came immediately. It was a warm evening in the middle of April, and perspiration dribbled from his sideburns down his dark brown cheeks. "What's wrong? You're all sweaty." "It's just that I hurried. I didn't want to keep you waiting." He said he should avoid sake and finally drank just one glass of beer.

"Shall we go see a movie?"

"Why don't we take a walk in Maruyama, instead, and look at the cherry blossoms by night?" Following Teramoto's suggestion, they strolled from Kyōgoku to Maruyama.

"Have you been riding?" he asked, as they climbed the stone steps at Gion and came to a dark spot.

"It was here that you gave me my first lessons, wasn't it? I haven't been riding at all these days. There are no horses nearby."

Teramoto was silent.

Now and then she deliberately brushed against the back of his hand.

"I gave you my address, but you never write to me."

"I thought it would be wrong to write too often, so I held back."

"Why? What's wrong with writing?"

"Nothing in particular,—I just held back . . ."

"But I'm happy today. I hadn't seen you for a long time, and I wondered if you'd come when I called."

"I've been seeing you in your pictures, though. I go to all of them that come to Kyoto."

"My pictures are boring—not one of them is any good."

"I've known you in pictures for a long time; I've been seeing them for three or four years." This was the first time Teramoto had confided such a thing.

"Really? But I wasn't in many pictures before, only five or six."

"I've seen two or three of them, anyway."

"You may see me in pictures, but it doesn't do any good, because I can't see you. You should become a movie actor."

"Maybe I'll go to work for Nikkatsu. I could ride a horse in action dramas."

"No, pictures aren't enough—I have to be with the real you."

Since he escorted her all the way back to the station at Shichijō, she said, "I'll be bored on the train; ride with me as far as Osaka," and Teramoto, though he worried about the time, went with her. When he said he would turn around and go right back, she pushed him into a taxi and they chatted for a while at the Nagahori Café, Teramoto looking at the clock all the while.

"Miss Mayuko, what time is your last train? Won't you be late?"

"That's all right—if I can't get home I don't mind going to a hotel."

"But I have to go back."

"Isn't there someplace you can stay in Osaka?"

"No, there isn't, and I have to go back anyway."

He stayed with her until exactly eleven-thirty and then took the last train home on the Keihan Electric line.

After that the image of Teramoto in his student uniform would pop into her mind from time to time, and something would make her desperate to see him. Presently she wrote that she would visit Kyoto again at the end of April. Meeting at the station at two o'clock, they went from Saga to Arashiyama. Teramoto was unusually lively. When she was about to break off a branch of double cherry blossoms, he cried, "Stop, thief!" Then he scrambled up the same tree and broke off a beautiful branch for her. They took a boat from Togetsu Bridge to the hot spring at Saga, where Teramoto treated her to dinner. "I want to stay at this hot spring tonight"—the words were on the tip of her tongue, but for some reason she could not speak them.

Teramoto's manner was just too bright and cheery for her to say such a thing. "Won't you come visit me sometime at Suikōen?" she said. "It'll be my turn to treat you to a meal." But Teramoto answered with a vague "Yes, thanks." She would ask when, and he would casually reply, "I'm rather busy these days" or "Before long, definitely" and change the subject.

I've never let a man get away before, once I set my sights on him—whether jewelry, clothing, or men, when I wanted something, I made it my own; and so why haven't I had my way with Teramoto? Have I fallen for him that hard? It's so irritating—and so foolish. But what does he mean by this letter? If he came on Sunday, Odagiri wouldn't be here, Onchi would be working late, and I'd be free all day—everything's in place, but he's slipped away again. Is it because of something I wrote in my letter the day before yesterday? "Please come as early as possible, by two o'clock, if you can. Only the two maids will be here, no one to make you feel constrained," I wrote. Was "no one to make you feel constrained" a blunder? Did he think it would be too risky to come? But surely he wouldn't lie; it's probably true that his father's in town. He says he'll find another time to visit me, and so I suppose he does want to come. Well, there's no hurry, as long as he comes soon, and even if he says he won't come, I'm not going to take no for an answer this time . . .

As these thoughts ran through Mayuko's head, she heard someone at the front door and then Onchi's voice saying, "Miyo, is your sister upstairs?" Apparently he discarded his Western clothes in the sitting room and went into the bath. Presently he came up the stairs wearing nothing but undershorts and an unlined serge kimono draped over his shoulders. "What a hot day! I'd like to splash around in that river outside!"

3

"Here, Onchi, look at this ring." Having hidden the letter in her sash when she heard his steps, she now held her fingers up to his face.

"Hmmm, is this the ring? The stone is a . . . a . . . aka . . . aka . . . , I give up, what do you call it?"

"Aquamarine. I just picked it up in Kobe. The stone's all right, but don't you think the gold is too reddish?"

"It's not red, it's just right. Expensive?"

"Take a guess."

"About fifty yen?"

"Less than that."

"Thirty, then."

"A little less."

"Twenty-five."

"Close enough."

"Really? That cheap?"

"Keep your opinions to yourself. It's not as if you could afford it."

"That's a fine way to talk." Putting his arms through the sleeves of his kimono, Onchi sat cross-legged on the veranda without tying his sash. "Now that you mention it, I need a hat. I'm embarrassed to be seen in that old one."

"Shall I buy one for you?"

"Please do, but I don't want a cheap one. Get me a soft felt Stetson."

"Don't be stupid. Everyone's wearing straw hats these days."

"I don't need you to buy straw hats for me; I'll get them myself. At one yen fifty, I'll buy a new hat every month and toss the old ones."

Sitting with the soles of his feet together, like the ancient aristocrats pictured on "One Hundred Poets, One Poem Each" cards, Onchi hugged his thighs as if he were unsure what to do with his long, thin legs. Though his skin was not particularly fair, he made good use of his graceful body, which had the look of a boy of seventeen or eighteen with alluring, light brown skin and trim, smooth musculature. He was always ready to slip off his kimono and display his body. He and Mayuko had known each other for some time, having first met in Tokyo; for a while they had an on-again-off-again relationship, and then both had come to western Japan because of the Tokyo earthquake, found themselves working at the same studio, and got back together again. Coming and going as if this were his own house, he had finally settled in a week before. They had been on familiar terms for a long time, but she realized now, as she looked at him, that she should not underestimate him; he had cute eyes. The tips of his fingers, as deft as a pianist's, carried a faint amber stain, probably from some coloring agent, which she found seductive. She could not understand why he had chosen to process film, given that he would be perfect in the role of a lover had he become an actor. He was perhaps a year older than Mayuko, or at least the same age, but knowing very well that his face retained a childlike winsomeness, he would sometimes wheedle and coax, which within the studio earned him a reputation as a phony; but his wheedling did not annoy Mayuko.

Beyond the veranda rail the sun was setting, and the sound of flowing water came to them with piercing clarity. There were no shadows anywhere, and the whiteness of the soil stood out, even in the dusk, so brightly that they could have counted the trunks of the little pines, one by one. Mayuko felt comfortable and relaxed, as if they were at some distant hot-spring inn. The business with Teramoto did not weigh on her mind. She had even forgotten that his letter was hidden in her sash. *Teramoto is a nuisance; if it won't work out with him, it won't work out. I'm not going to get upset about something that won't come about soon, anyway. The man I'm with now is plenty. As far as I'm concerned, he's much more* schön *than Teramoto, and he knows my disposition inside and out . . .*

"The Old Man's coming today."

"I know. And I'll be shooed downstairs again. It's too much to bear."

They paused in their conversation when O-miyo brought up the evening paper.

"Where are the nail scissors?" Onchi helped himself to the vanity case that lay on the table, extracted the scissors, spread the newspaper on the veranda, and began to trim his toenails.

"Onchi, come upstairs tonight, will you?"

"Why?"

"It would be better that way. O-miyo and O-moto will be downstairs."

"What time?"

"Two-thirty or three. I'll switch on the light at the stairs when the time is right. Come up when the light is on."

"Where do you want me?"

"In there." Mayuko pointed with her chin to the adjoining six-mat room.

"Are you sure it'll be all right?"

"He always falls sound asleep. I give him Adalin."[1]

"Does he know?"

"He can't tell. I have my ways."

"That's nasty!" said Onchi, using a local expression he had picked up recently. He put down the scissors.

It was about seven-thirty when Odagiri arrived, wearing a lined Ōshima kimono with a silk-gauze summer *haori* and pongee *hakama*; an ivory knob capped his walking stick, a meerschaum pipe was clamped between his jaws, and, as was his habit, he walked deliberately, stomping his feet like a sumo wrestler.

"Welcome," said O-miyo, bowing at the entryway, but Odagiri just grunted and went straight upstairs, as if he were embarrassed about something. Before long O-miyo announced that the water was hot; Odagiri and Mayuko spent nearly an hour in the bath. When they emerged, they ensconced themselves again on the second floor, had dinner trays brought up, and the drinking began. Downstairs O-miyo could hear no clattering or conversation from above, and

---

1. Adalin (carbromal) is a sedative and hypnotic, originally synthesized by Bayer.

she certainly would not go up unless she were called. Nevertheless, Mayuko and Odagiri apparently consumed quite a lot of alcohol, for, though they rarely had Japanese sake, they would always drink Château Larose or chablis with the meal, and after dinner they would imbibe Courvoisier cognac or liqueurs while they nibbled on cheese. Odagiri himself obtained these Western beverages from Kobe by special order and always kept Mayuko's house well stocked.

"Hey! Miyo! Is Onchi down there?" Mayuko's shriek came from upstairs about an hour into their customary after-dinner drinks. Onchi was at the table with O-miyo and O-moto, eating from a pot of *hamo* eel sukiyaki. He cried "Yes!", tossed his chopsticks aside, and bounded to the foot of the stairs.

Mayuko looked down at him. "Have you had dinner?"

"We are eating now," Onchi replied politely. "I have almost finished. What can I do for you?"

"Would you come upstairs when you've eaten? Papa-san says he'll treat you to an unusual drink."

"Thank you! I'll take a quick bath first."

"You can bathe later, can't you?"

"It'll only take five or ten minutes, really. I won't be able to get in the water after if I'm drunk."

"And who said they'd give you enough to make you drunk?"

"Oops, that was a blunder, wasn't it?"

"Quit your dawdling and get up here. Now!"

"All right, I'll take a bath later."

Onchi hurried back to the sitting room, wolfed down the rest of his rice, retied his sash, and went upstairs.

"Excuse me for barging in, I've come for a treat . . . Mayuko, say something for me. I'm no good at these formalities."

"What are you talking about," Mayuko said with a titter. "Why be so proper? You've met before, haven't you?"

"Well, yes, but . . ."

"Hello, it's been a while, hasn't it?" Odagiri finally spoke. "When did you come to this part of the country?"

"In February this year. We've crossed paths now and then since then, but I failed to greet you properly. I'm sorry." Onchi put a hand on the back of his neck and gave a quick bow.

"Here, which do you want, cognac or liqueur?"

"Either one would be fine."

"Don't stand on ceremony when he says he'll treat you. Papa-san, you tell him."

"Yes, really, there's no need to be reserved."

"All right, then, let me try both. I've never tasted either one."

In fact he had already sneaked a cupful of each.

Though he had invited Onchi upstairs with an offer of liquor, Odagiri left all the entertaining to Mayuko and, though he was not in a bad mood, listened to their chatter sullenly and silently. Onchi, who was not at all bashful, took secret pride in the fact that everyone seemed to like him, but he felt ill at ease in Odagiri's company, not knowing what to make of the man. *What does he think of Mayuko and me? Does he know about our relationship or not?* It did not sit right with him. "Well, he's probably figured it out, don't you think? But there are twenty years between me and the Old Man, and he's resigned to reality." So Mayuko had said, but the way Odagiri watched a person with that strange, ill-natured look in his eye somehow got on Onchi's nerves. What is more, Mayuko might call him "Papa-san" and "the Old Man," but with his calm, plump appearance, he cut a fine, gentlemanly figure and looked no more than forty, which was three or four years younger than his real age. In fact he must truly like Mayuko since she said he was no match for her and would let her get away with anything; but there had been no talk of jealousy—was he cunning or was he putting on airs?—and in his complete submission to her, he seemed to be too susceptible to women to be believed. When they had been in Tokyo, too, men had come and gone openly, but Odagiri was always bighearted, never complaining, as if to say these visits were only to be expected when one had an actress as his mistress. Onchi had not heard before that Odagiri was being given adalin unknowingly; but he had heard from the actors

H and Y, when they were talking about their love lives, that they had spent the night under the same roof as Odagiri and performed similar mischief while Mayuko was living in the Meguro district of Tokyo. For a time there had also been talk that Odagiri might have a taste for handsome boys and that he acquiesced to Mayuko's affairs because he enjoyed the company of these boys. On the subject of Onchi's showing up at the doorstep, Mayuko had even said, "Don't worry about it. The Old Man likes handsome boys, and he says you're *schön*." In any case, Odagiri was a strange man. Even when they were sitting face-to-face, he said nothing to Onchi. He seemed to be affecting an air of composure since it would be comical for a man his age to have a fondness for boys; and even as he glared at Onchi, he seemed to be pretending that he liked him, for fear of displeasing Mayuko, when in fact he considered him a shameless scoundrel. *It makes no difference; if I'm shameless, go ahead and think I'm shameless.* Thus Onchi had mustered his courage. He was good at reading people's faces, but he would not know how to deal with Odagiri if he could not be sure on this point. It was fine to be offered a drink, but he was not enjoying the taste. The alcohol went straight to his head, his neck flushed hotly, and he felt as if he were suffocating under some strange pressure.

"Papa-san, Papa-san, which is more *schön*—Onchi or H?"

Just as Onchi was thinking he could stand it no longer, Mayuko blurted this out and threw him a sidelong glance.

"You remember H, don't you, Papa-san? That kid who used to visit when I lived in Meguro?"

It was her habit to refer to all her young men as "kids." Onchi, too, was a "kid" behind his back.

"Umm . . ."

"Who is more *schön*, Papa-san? H or Onchi?"

"Hmm, I wonder . . ." Odagiri sounded annoyed as he mumbled this, but at the same time his eyes, full of curiosity and yet strangely timid, glanced furtively at the handsome youth sitting across the table from him. When their eyes met, however, he abruptly looked away and began to gaze fondly at the movement of Mayuko's hands and feet, at her cheeks, and at her neck. His look had the voracity of a tongue and seemed to be saying, "How about this woman! Doesn't she have a beautiful body—soft, sleek, as lissome as gentle waves? That's why I love her."

"So which is it? I think Onchi is more *schön*."

"You . . . you must be joking," said Onchi, his hand on the back of his neck again. "H is much more *schön*. I can't come close."

"Liar! And you're so conceited!"

"Hey! You astonish me!"

"He says your talents are wasted as a film processor."

"Who says?"

"Papa-san."

"What?" Once again Onchi felt those eyes staring at him, brimming with curiosity. When he glanced up, he was amazed to see Odagiri blush like a maiden.

"That's right, isn't it Papa-san? Onchi is your favorite. Don't you remember saying so?"

Odagiri seemed to grunt in agreement, but Onchi was aware only of a slight movement in the evasive man's lips.

4

"Stop pestering me! I told you to stop, and here you come again!"

"But . . . but . . ."

"But what! Stupid Old Man! Everyone can see us from outside."

"No they can't; no one's passing by at this time of night."

"You never know who might be watching us, or from where! They even built a house in the middle of that pine grove."

"But it's on the other side of the river."

"That doesn't mean they can't see us. It's pitch dark out there, and the second floor here is all lit up."

"Then let's close the doors. Call O-miyo and have her close the doors."

"No, if we close the doors now it'll get all hot and stuffy in here."

"But it's already midnight."

"What's wrong with that? I want to stay out here a little longer and enjoy the cool air."

"You'll catch cold, wearing such thin material."

"Who cares? Mind your own business. Have another drink, Papa-san."

About ten minutes had elapsed since Onchi went downstairs. Sprawled on the rattan chaise longue, Mayuko had propped one arm on the veranda rail and let the other hang beyond the arm rest; she extended her legs luxuriantly, with the overlapping skirts of her kimono pressed tightly between them, as if she were wearing trousers. Squatting on a cushion he had placed on the threshold between the veranda and the room, and staying behind the chaise so he could not be seen from the garden, Odagiri squeezed Mayuko's hand as it dangled from above. As always when they were alone together, he could not rest unless he was constantly stroking the skin on one part of Mayuko's body or another; when she showed her annoyance, he would be satisfied even with her fingertips or the sole of a foot. She had long since grown used to this behavior, but recently Odagiri had grown especially persistent, so that she felt as though a fly were endlessly crawling over her body. Sometimes her temper would flare.

"Let go of my hand! Do you always have to be squeezing it?"

"But what's the harm in . . ."

"Stop," she said harshly. "I hate it!" Shaking him off, she hid her hand inside the lapels of her kimono, as if it were some rarely displayed article.

Slithering toward the foot of the chaise, Odagiri caressed her ankle, and his fingers crept to her toes.

"This man!—Dog! Old-man dog!" The skirt of her kimono lifted suddenly and her foot delivered an abrupt kick to Odagiri's forehead. Even so, Odagiri did not stop.

Accepting that there was nothing she could do about it, Mayuko let him play with her feet while she looked down on his head from the chaise. One would not notice it from looking at his face, but—was he getting old?—seen from above, he was starting to go bald. There was something sad about the way he always fussed with his hair, smearing it with Eau de Quinine, applying Brilliantine, and keeping it in place with bandoline. For that matter, did he not already have the body of an old man? Look at that soft plumpness, the flabby, unsightly fleshiness around his neck and shoulders, creased here and there with lines like an infant's wrist. How could it compare with the firm-skinned "youthfulness" of Teramoto and Onchi? At some point this person she always called "Old Man" really had begun to turn into an old man. But while he was growing old, she, too, was putting on years. Next year she would be twenty-four, the year after that twenty-five . . . If she went on dawdling, she would turn thirty before she knew it. She did not want to go on forever as an underpaid actress. Why must the man have this unfortunate temperament? If he shaped up, he would be a splendid man, one you could depend on, but this strange quirk of his only got worse as he aged and showed no sign of going away . . .

Tears formed in her eyes, imperceptible both to the man under the chaise and to Mayuko herself. Once again she cried angrily, "Stupid Old Man!" and kicked Odagiri. As she kicked him again, and again, and again, she became aware of something trickling down her cheeks, but she made no move to wipe it away.

"Old Man! Pour me a liqueur."

As he filled her glass, Odagiri looked up at her face, unexpectedly wet with dew; a weird, embarrassed grin creased his cheeks.

Mayuko was innately wayward and tomboyish, but it was Odagiri who exacerbated these tendencies beyond what she was born with. It had been four or five years before, when she was eighteen or nineteen and working as a dancing girl in a Shanghai café, that Odagiri had fallen for her; and, in retrospect, it was because certain characteristics—her impishness, her reckless, rough way of speaking, and her fashionably bobbed hair—had agreed with the man's unwholesome tastes. Mayuko herself had been unaware of this at the time. She had taken him for a rich man with a pampered upbringing and a weakness for women, a man who was completely smitten with her. Even after she became his mistress, she had secretly indulged in whatever mischief she pleased. It amused her to keep him at her beck and call while she deceived him, and possessing the skill to do so was pleasant. But recently, as she gradually came to understand the man's secrets more clearly, she had realized that, even as she thought she was deceiving him, in fact she was being forced into a mold of his design—that her flesh and even her personality were being toyed with.

Odagiri had been her patron in the years since then, but she had never felt the constraints implied by the words "I have a patron." He had never once been jealous, for all that he kept such a self-indulgent woman. Now and then he had made a pretense of jealousy, but it was nothing more than an act calculated to satisfy his perverse desires. Everything the man did was an act. He was no fool, but he played the role of a fool; he was not deceived, but he pretended to be deceived; normally a respectable man, he grew timid before her and wheedled like a whimpering woman—as a man who derived an inexpressible joy from such playacting, and from nothing else, he had no intention of loving anyone sincerely, nor any wish to be sincerely loved. He was a man who rejoiced in being called "Old Man," not "dear," and in being kicked around, not caressed; who would rather be treated like a blockhead than have his woman remain faithful to him; who preferred the role of a clown to that of a lover. At first this had only amused her, and she had even found it convenient for her own purposes; but when the crazed look in his eyes grew more obvious, as it had recently done, it became clear to her that he was not in love with her, that she had become his slave even as she behaved like a queen, that she had been incited and gone too far, and before she knew it she was being used as a perverse tool; and with this realization sometimes came a sudden, overwhelming loneliness.

It was around one o'clock when O-miyo came upstairs, briefly swept the room again, and closed the storm shutters.

Lazy and weary, perhaps from the effects of her one glass of liqueur, Mayuko made no move to rise from the chaise while O-miyo straightened things up and arranged the bedding.

"Don't bother with me; help your big sister with her nightgown," Odagiri was saying.

Fastidious and well groomed, O-miyo did not smell of perspiration, but her dry, shriveled hands and feet; her misshapen, angular face; her little eyes, peering shrewdly from among her freckles; her protruding chin and large mouth; her nostrils, so tiny one marveled that air could pass through them—the hunchbacked O-miyo nevertheless worked well and meticulously; but now Mayuko could imagine why Odagiri had shown pity for O-miyo, had repeatedly urged Mayuko to help her "crippled cousin," and had wished to install her in the house. Odagiri was always encouraging Mayuko to keep an animal. When they had seen Barbara La Marr's *Trifling Women* at the Shōchiku Theater in Dōtombori, he had said, "Why don't you get a monkey, too? That monkey makes Barbara La Marr look even more voluptuous. It's good for a movie actress to have a monkey." Mayuko refused, but he kept trying to persuade her. Then, after O-miyo's arrival, he let O-miyo take care of everything related to Mayuko's body that he did not do himself. Combing her hair, polishing her nails, scrubbing her back, massaging her legs and feet, putting on and taking off her shoes—Mayuko did not enjoy doing anything for herself, and so the psychologically crippled Odagiri and the physically crippled O-miyo saw to it together that their mistress need not lift a finger. *O-miyo, too, is one of Odagiri's tools. Not only me, but everyone around me is a tool in his hands as well—O-miyo, H, Onchi . . .*

"Do you want to change?" O-miyo mumbled from behind the chaise, where she had been waiting for some time with Mayuko's nightgown.

Finally Mayuko rose and began to loosen her sash. "Wait a minute," she said, suddenly remembering. She searched inside her kimono and in the sleeves. She had forgotten where she put Teramoto's letter.

"It was in the bathroom; I hid it," O-miyo whispered in her ear.

Replying with a nod, Mayuko slipped off her kimono and put her hands through the sleeves of the *yukata* as O-miyo held it open behind her . . . Not for the first time, Mayuko felt something ominous in the thought that O-miyo, though she kept quiet, knew everything. Odagiri's secrets, her mistress's heart, her own position—all these were perfectly clear to her, were they not? . . .

O-miyo picked up the flannel from the floor of the veranda, draped it over a bamboo hanger, and folded the sash. "Good-night," she said, and went downstairs.

5

In the darkness that dimly covered the lamp, Odagiri snored, perhaps under the influence of Adalin, perhaps playing possum.

Mayuko tried moving slightly. Then she pushed aside an arm that was in her way. The momentum slid the arm off the pillow, but she did not sense any reaction from Odagiri. There was a childlike innocence in the way his mouth hung open, and he seemed about to drool.

Has he really gone to sleep? This lunatic?

For a time she gazed suspiciously at his face in sleep. He was quite audacious about feigning sleep. When they were still in Meguro, he had known when H and Y came sneaking in. This, too, was an act, and assuming the role was one of his secret pleasures. "I appreciate *schön* like him; why don't you let him stay here?" he had said, and after Onchi had begun to spend the night recently, she sometimes gave Adalin to Odagiri. She would chew up one, two, or three half-gram tablets and give them to him mouth to mouth. He would swallow happily. He probably fantasized that she was administering poison. When she did this for him, Odagiri would submit to all her demands the next morning. Sometimes it would be extra spending money; sometimes he would order a new kimono for her. He had been the first to drop a hint about this, and a sort of agreement had been reached between them before they knew it. It was not entirely a bad deal for Mayuko, but, always tempted by lust and greed, she played into his hands.

Tonight she gave him five tablets. Then she mixed some cognac in hot water and had him drink three teacups full, but she still doubted that he was really asleep. She quietly turned back the quilt and got up. Sitting by the pillow with one knee drawn up, she grazed his face with her toes. Often this was enough to unmask his deception, since he was a maniacal foot worshipper, but these days he had grown cunning and treacherous and did not easily show his true colors. Two or three times she pressed the bottom of her big toe against his cheek and lips. He went on sleeping peacefully with his mouth hanging open.

Inch by inch, like a timid cat, Mayuko backed away from the enigmatic face. Stepping into the corridor, she switched on the light at the stairs.

Two eyes shone below. Onchi was already sitting on the steps.

"Onchi . . ."

" . . ."

"I really like you, I like you much more than before, you're my only love-san . . . Hey, Onchi!"

"Uh, yeah . . ."

She was weeping silently tonight. What could be the matter, Onchi wondered.

"You mustn't leave me, promise you'll never, never leave me."

"All right, all right."

"Do you promise, then?"

"Yeah."

"You won't play around?"

"And what about you?

"Certainly not, . . . if that's the way it's going to be."

"How can I trust you?"

"If you don't play around, neither will I. I'm not that kind of woman. I, I . . . , it's the Old Man who made me so bad."

"Quiet, quiet, you'll wake him up in the next room."

"Don't you feel sorry for me? I may look happy, but I'm the unhappiest person in the world. I've never told anyone before, being the kind of person I am, but I like you and suddenly I want to tell you everything. Is it wrong of me to say that?"

"Tomorrow. Let's talk tomorrow."

"No, tonight. I want to talk tonight."

"But what if he's listening?"

"I don't care! If he wants to listen, let him listen. The old pervert! . . . If you're serious, Sabu-chan, I'll explain everything to the Old Man and break up with him. Marry me, Onchi."

"On sixty yen a month? You don't mind starving to death?"

"You make sixty, I make two hundred. We can get by on that, can't we? I won't be extravagant. I'll turn my salary over to you. All right? Onchi?"

What's this woman saying? The weather will change again tomorrow.

"Yeah, it's all right; it's too good."

"Then, you agree?"

"Yeah, but you . . ."

"But what?"

". . . Well, you should . . ."

"Think it over? Is that what you mean?"

"Discuss it with Mr. Odagiri first, and . . ."

"I know that much. All right, if I break up with Odagiri, will you agree?"

"I will."

"You promise?"

"I promise."

"Hook your little finger with me."

"Right."

"There, we've linked fingers. OK?"

"Definitely."

"Thank-you, thank-you, Onchi . . . Is it funny if I cry?"

"No, . . . It makes you more adorable to think you have a soft spot, too."

"I'm a crybaby, actually, I can't bear it if you don't care for me . . ."

Mayuko wept on and on, clinging tightly to the young man.

6

Even though she was dozing, Mayuko remembered everything until dawn, when O-miyo came upstairs to slide open the shutters; but when the cold morning air drifted in, she fell into a comfortable, sound sleep.

"Sister . . ." It was some hours later that she heard the voice calling to her from beyond the shoji.

"Sister."

"Hmm?" Mayuko finally replied, still half asleep.

"You have a visitor."

"Who?"

"I have his card. May I open the door?" From the next room, O-miyo slid open the door by Mayuko's pillow and held out a calling card.

"Him?"

"Yes."

Teramoto! He said he couldn't come; I wonder what happened. And today isn't Sunday—has he come all the way from Kyoto? It doesn't matter, I'm glad he's here. There must be some reason . . . Mayuko quickly dragged herself across the tatami and reached for Odagiri's watch. It was already past ten o'clock. And what about the Old Man? He had said he would return to Osaka at ten in the morning, but he was still asleep. Unaware that the sun was beating in from around the shoji, he seemed to be sound asleep, now that he no longer needed to be.

His face was covered with clammy sweat, and the crumpled quilt lay horizontally across his protruding belly.

"I'll go downstairs right away." Glancing contemptuously at the sleeping figure, Mayuko sprang up, changed her kimono, tied her sash, touched up her face, and rushed down to the front door.

"What a surprise!"

"Hello! Forgive me for dropping in like this."

He looked up at her with his strong, masculine eyes. This was the lively Teramoto who had taken her to Arashiyama.

"I'm so glad you came!"

"My father and sister said they were going to Arima Hot Springs today, so I escorted them as far as Takarazuka, then came here. I thought it would be rude to call on you unexpectedly, but since I had already come that far, I decided to drop by."

"That's fine, it's no problem at all."

"But you'll be going to the studio, won't you?"

"There'll be no shoots for two or three days, so I can take some time off. Please stay for a while . . . I'll just straighten up the second floor."

"Shall I take a walk while you're doing that?"

The white earth glared in the sunshine beyond the lattice door, and in the reflected light inside the entry, the walking stick with its ivory knob protruded from a ceramic umbrella stand. Thinking that Teramoto must have seen it, Mayuko grew fretful.

"It's OK, you don't need to take a walk! I'm just going to straighten things up a little, it won't take five minutes!"

"Really? In that case . . ." Teramoto hesitated.

"All right? Don't go anywhere! Wait here." She closed the shoji firmly.

"Miyo, come upstairs with me." She ran up the steps.

"Old Man! Get up! Get up!"

"Um, ah, let me . . . let me sleep a little more."

"I can't. Get up and go home!" Kicking the pillow aside, she raised his heavy head by the earlobes.

"Ow! Ow!"

"Does that hurt? Are you awake, then? Here, get up, get up!"

"But why . . ."

"Never mind why. I told you to get up! Get up, change into your kimono, and go! I have an important guest."

"Who is it?"

"Never mind who. Someone you don't know.—Miyo, go ahead and put away the bedding!"

"You amaze me. If it's someone I don't know, you should introduce me."

"Idiot! He's not that kind of person! Here! Put on your kimono! Be quick about it!"

"Wait a minute, I have to wash my face."

"Wash your face somewhere else! I won't let you wash here today."

"Wh . . . why?"

"Because I can't stand to have you and him in the same house together."

"It's all right for Onchi to be here?"

"What are you talking about? What time do you think it is? He left for work hours ago. You worm! Hurry up and go, I said!"

"But I just want to take a little bitty look at him."

"Forget it. If you saw him he'd be contaminated.—Miyo, I'm going to keep an eye on the Old Man and take him down to the sitting room. After that, send the guest up here to the second floor."

"The gentleman's hat and *hakama* are still here . . ."

"Give them to me. After you've sent the guest upstairs, move the Old Man's clogs around to the garden side of the house."

She pulled him up again by the earlobes. "All right? If you say anything on the way downstairs, I'll never forgive you. We're going to the sitting room and you're going to keep quiet. Otherwise I won't let you come near this house again."

"What a dreadful experience!" Odagiri finally spoke while pulling on his *hakama* in the sitting room.

"What's wrong with having a dreadful experience? That's what you like, isn't it, Papa-san? Now leave two hundred yen with me before you go."

"Could you make it one hundred?"

"No. Two hundred. I gave you all that adalin last night, didn't I? And I bought a ring. I don't have a penny."

Reluctantly he pulled two hundred-yen notes from his billfold. Mayuko snatched them from him, folded them in four, and rolled them up in her hand.

"Now leave as I watch you. Your clogs are over there."

"My walking stick, my stick, I forgot my stick."

"Your stick is fine where it is. I'll keep it for you until the next time you come."

"But why?"

"Because it would look funny if something that was in the entryway before isn't there later. Go home today without it."

Odagiri scrambled from the sitting room veranda down into the garden.

"Mr. Teramoto. I'm sorry I kept you waiting."

Coming upstairs two or three minutes later, trembling with anticipation, Mayuko glimpsed Odagiri's back as he moved through the pine grove, on the far side of the river, toward the station. Without his walking stick, the Old Man seemed unsure what to do with his hands, but, as always, he walked deliberately, stomping his feet like a sumo wrestler.

ABOUT THE TRANSLATORS

Paul McCarthy is Professor Emeritus, Surugadai University, Saitama, Japan.

Anthony H. Chambers is Professor Emeritus of Japanese at Arizona State University.